THESE FORGOTTEN MOUNTAIN MEN OMNIBUS

WHISPERED ECHOES

SOFIA AVES

First Edition

PRINT ISBN 978-1-923471-97-9

FORGOTTEN
MOUNTAIN MAN

WHISPERED ECHOES
SERIES

USA TODAY BEST SELLING AUTHOR

SOFIA AVES

PLAYLIST

Bar None - Jordan Davis
Caroline - Mumford & Sons
Afterlife - Evanescence
Worlds Apart - Marshmallow, AR/CO
Sunshine & Rain - Kali Uchis
Casino - Tucker Wetmore
We Don't Talk - The Dreggs
Carry Me Through - Maren Morris
Backroad of my Mind - Ryan Jesse
Forever Overdose - Amira Elfeky
Dirty Money - Travis Collins
LOVELIFE - Sam Fischer

FORGOTTEN MOUNTAIN MAN

I've spent years hiding from a world that's best forgotten me. I'm a man who prefers the company of the wind to my own kind. Strangers are never welcome.

When a woman who should never have crossed into my territory decides to set up house right on my doorstep, I'm forced to endure the calamity she brings with her. My existence is upended by a redhead tornado hellbent on destroying the peace I've garnered in the remotest corner of Montana.

By the time I've accepted her changes in my life it's too late...I've fallen for the girl who dared poke the proverbial bear. But she's brought a secret to my mountains that means leaving my hidden corner of the world or risk losing everything I've found with the girl who healed me.

For all the times you wanted to be forgotten—really forgotten, but then wanted that one person to come and find you?
There's a story for that.

CHAPTER ONE

FAITH

"You're going up *where* in *what*?" Jude looked at my car over my shoulder and managed to suppress his laughter. "Take one of the farm trucks, please, Faith, or I'll be scraping you off the mountain when the deluge hits in a few hours." The foreman of Red Hart Ranch waved a tanned hand toward a row of dusty, branded red and white pickups parked in a neat row out the front of the big house.

I plastered a smile on my face that had bore down on much lesser men than Jude Mannering—and much less well-mannered ones, too.

"No thank you, sir," I declined politely. "Me and Pretty Betty are going to trundle on up that little hill, give our papers to one Mister Walker Roan, and be back before the sun sets."

I pointed to the manilla folder fat with a sheaf of files stuffed inside where it perched on the passenger seat of my ancient bubble car. Long overdue for replacement since I graduated college, I still hadn't upgraded my ride despite opening my own office in White cap, a few hours' drive south of Red Hart. Maybe I should after this. One last road trip in Pretty Betty for my current client.

Or rather, my late client's son.

"Are you still driving that beat up old thing, Faith? Betty hasn't given out on you yet?" Travis Beaumont, co-owner of Red Hart with his twin sister, Eve, stomped down the wide front steps of the big house, banging his black hat on his denim covered thigh. "You know a girl should spoil herself when she has her name plastered in big letters in the main street."

He leaned down from his six-foot, six-inches height to engulf me in a bear hug where I nearly died from lack of oxygen within seconds.

"Letting that same girl breathe helps," I huffed at him, slapping his shoulders with my hands on his back where I could reach.

"Oops." Travis sent me an apologetic grin. "I do

the same thing to my wife sometimes. She's almost as small as you."

I snorted. "Bet she doesn't grumble."

His cheeks pinked. "Yeah..."

Jude coughed into his fist, and the sound was fake as all hell. "Still holding to my point, Fatih. With those clouds closing in, you shouldn't be going up the mountain. Not today."

I stared at the fluffy white peaks that decorated the imposing peaks behind Red Hart's big house in a pretty ring. "I can still see the summit, Jude. Seriously?" I eyed Travis, waiting on the landowner to weigh in. Not that I didn't trust Jude, just that...

Okay, so the ranch foreman was known to be overprotective with pretty much everyone who crossed the land he considered his to protect by right. And I knew he was being a sweetheart, but he also hated leaving ranch land. I was about to cross well beyond anything that was considered Red Hart boundaries, even though I'd spend a good half hour driving right across the eastern boundary to enter the next territory.

Which was where I'd find Walker Roan. Eventually.

My client passed away over two years ago and I'd been emailing, messaging, calling and finally snail mailing his son since then to clear up the little matter of his twenty freaking million dollar inheritance that had been burning a hole right through my desk that entire time.

Anyone else would have been dying to get their hands on the patch of prime Montana land on the outskirts of White Cap. Anyone, apparently, except Walker Roan.

Now, it was time to collect, for both of us.

Walker Roan wouldn't be able to ignore me when I turned up on his doorstep. Not this time.

Travis kicked up dust bunnies with the toe of his boot. "I dunno that heading up the mountain is such a good idea, Faith. Maybe wait til one of the boys can take you. If you hold out until next week, then Eve or I can go with you. Make a picnic date of it and we can all catch up together?" Hope lit his eyes.

I hated dashing it in one.

"Not you, too?" I placed a hand on his arm. "Is this even about the weather?"

The boys exchanged glances over my head. I stomped my heel in the dirt. "Don't do that. I am *not* insignificant just because I'm a foot and a half shorter than everyone here."

Jude snorted and ruffled my hair, the sweetheart–asshole. "No, you're far from insignificant,

Faith," he rumbled. "But we worry about you. No one's seen Walker in..."

"A while," Travis put in softly. "I don't know that he's in any sort of consumable human state. Not for you. For all we know he's turned into a cactus up there," he tacked a joke onto the end of his anti-Faith-mountain-date-spiel.

A crap one.

I glared at him. "I don't need Roan to be in a consumable state. I just need him to say yay or fucking nay, sign or come back with me, and the deal is done."

"He won't come back with you," the boys chorused like twins.

I raised my eyebrows. "You two married the wrong people. Thanks for the heads up. And the coffee." I hugged Eve as she trotted down the steps holding an oversized coffee thermos.

"I wasn't about to send you off unarmed." She hugged me back and produced a container of assorted home cooked slices out of nowhere. "Plus, in case it really does close in and you get stuck. You need to turn around, there's always a bed for you here. And Kyle is about on the other side of the mountain if you need help in that direction. Not that there's any reception once you hit the boundary."

She frowned and winced all in the space of a second. Her hand dropped to her hip and she squeezed inward.

It was my turn to worry about her. "Are you okay?"

"Fine." She brushed off my concern with a tired smile. "Perimenopause hitting in five years too early. Hot sweats have started too."

I stared. "You are way too young for that. Have you been to the doctor?"

"Too many times to count. Do you have enough fuel? Got jerry cans?"

I blinked. "I hadn't thought—"

"Walker has a stash, assuming it hasn't all gone stale. Been a long damn time since he was in town," Jude muttered. "I can get you something." He eyed my trunk. "Make your car stink, though."

"No, thank you. Pretty Betty shalt not stink. The car commandments." I hefted my lunch container and my coffee thermos over my head to increase my height before the predators crowding around me and air kissed Eve. "Look after yourself," I whispered. "I'll be back soon, with Walker."

Her eyes sparkled with my impending mischief. "I can't wait."

Then I was gone in a flurry of dust bunnies

bigger than the ones that Travis kicked up, headed for Red Hart's eastern boundary where I would find Walker Roan and finally get his oversized, over-stuffed and long overdue file off my otherwise clean desk.

CHAPTER TWO

WALKER

I planted my feet shoulder width apart and tried to ignore the sound of the tinny engine noise that reverberated along my spine crept up the mountain. Not that I expected anyone—Jude knew better than to head up my way when rain was due, and I hadn't capped the drive like I promised myself I would months ago when the rain last stopped.

Now, it looked like I'd be doing a whole lot more when the remainder of last year's effort washed away in a few hours' time and left me with a slippery granite slope that wouldn't be drivable any time soon.

Not that I cared if I was stuck up on the mountain for a while longer. I had no plans on leaving. Whoever decided to visit, however, might object to my personal habits when they were stuck here with me. I hadn't shared my living space with another human for some time.

The clunky sound choked just outside my line of sight. I frowned, my axe lifted over my head as I stared down at the round of timber set out before me. That pathetic, rusty little vehicle didn't sound anything like any of the Red Hart trucks, and it sure as hell didn't belong to anything that trader Kyle might drive.

I placed my axe against the giant larch stump I habitually used for chopping rounds. With clouds setting in well after midday, I had a need for dry wood. Once the rain started on my side of the mountain, it tended not to stop for a while.

Exhaling a long breath I swung about to face the newcomer invading my rocky granite outcrop where I'd made my home just over a decade ago when I left White Cap. Travis' father offered me a home back then when my own refused to do the same. I took the offer, and his son and his best friend worked shoulder to shoulder beside me for a season to help build a simple log cabin just big enough to keep the snow off my back in winter.

I'd stayed here ever since, only coming down to the big house to top up supplies and fuel when the jenny ran dry.

Which was why an unannounced visitor at this time of year with rain pending was not my idea of a good time.

I cast an eye heavenward just as a ratty little white car that probably should have stayed in White Cap about the same time as I left the small Montana town butted its scarred hood over the edge of my drive and onto the plateau where I spent my hours. The vehicle announced its presence with a death rattle that could have woken half the mountain range, and died.

The driver didn't seem deterred at all by the steam that billowed in plumes from where I assumed the little car kept what remained of its engine. She bounded out of her car, red hair swinging from her shoulders to her—holy shit, did those sunset colored locks actually hang all the way to her *knees*? Dressed in white jeans that stopped mid-calf and a red knitted top that bared her shoulders, neither my mountain nor myself had seen anything as vibrant as this tiny woman in years, if ever.

Not that the woman was tall; she'd be lucky to

reach my nipples if we stood forehead to chest level. But her hair was fairytale length at least. Considering her dramatic arrival, I wondered if I shouldn't be on the lookout for a wicked stepmother, or perhaps a wayward dragon on the fly.

"Walker Roan." Her voice stopped me dead as she stalked toward me, tapping a manilla folder as thick as my forearm in her hands. A sultry smile curved cherrywood red lips to match her hair. "You are not an easy man to catch, sir." She smiled and tossed the folder on the hood of her car—for dramatic effect, I suspected.

Damn slip of a thing would be lucky if those papers didn't blow away and end up at the bottom of the mountain in the next few minutes, the way the clouds were starting to roll in behind her, not that I expected she had noticed.

Something about the way my name rolled off her tongue left me hotter under the collar than a downslope wind rushing along the mountain face. I raked one hand through my beard, covering my mouth as I stared down at her. The woman didn't stop until the toes of her glossy patent heels—*who the fuck wore goddam high heels on their way up a mountain?*—touched my scuffed leather boots.

Yep, nipple level. Maybe an inch or so below. *Called it.*

That was where the top of her head reached on me as I stared down into her hazel color change eyes that matched the forest around us with their stunning array of greens and browns and yellows that shifted with the sunlight.

Those eyes that still watched me like she expected an answer.

Because she did.

I cleared my throat. "You're the woman who's been asking around about me, are you?" My voice came out rough, like I hadn't used it in a while.

She was my father's lawyer. Attorney. Whatever. Jude mentioned her at least once in the last six months, maybe sometime earlier. It wasn't like I kept track.

And she looked at me like my voice came out strange compared to what she was used to. Hell if I knew what the kids down at White Cap looked and sounded like. It's not like I had regular company up here, which was kind of the point. I supposed that unless I counted yelling *"Fuck!"* at the generator when I dropped my screwdriver between the panels at the back last month, it had been a while since I spoke to anyone.

"I'm Faith Somerset. We have a lot to talk about." Her hands planted on her hips and her gaze transformed into a glare in the space of seconds.

I could have sworn flame tried to roast me, too.

"Do we." I cleared my throat again and coughed when my voice itched, but the two words still came out flat as fuck.

Faith looked less than impressed. "I called, I emailed, and I messaged. Hell, I even sent you a freaking letter." Her voice rose at that last one with indignation.

I offered her a gentle smile to lessen the blow. "My post box is in White Cap. I haven't been in to clean it out in years. Trav has, though."

She stared at me. As I watched that glossy, patent heel on her left foot actually rose a few inches in slow motion then stamped back down in the epitome of a perfect, spoiled temper tantrum.

"Do you mean to tell me—" She inhaled a long, calming breath that seemed to do shit all for her, but it sure was amusing to me. "—that Travis Beaumont could have told me he's been collecting your mail for you all this time, right before I drove all the way up your fucking mountain?"

I smirked. "For a pretty little thing, you sure have a potty mouth. It's cute."

Her face pinked on cue. *Also cute.* "I. Am. Not. Little. Or cute," she added as an afterthought.

I let her have that one. "Didn't Travis tell you not to come up here with the weather closing in?" I asked.

Her glare returned. "He told me you never came off the mountain. I'm here to change your mind."

Her declaration didn't do shit for me. "You might want to move your car before the rain starts."

"What rain?"

A fat drop plopped right on the middle of her pert, ski-jump nose, washing away half her makeup in a second flat.

"That rain."

The deluge started as the sky that had been clear a second before darkened. Clouds that had been hiding around the western face of the mountain swirled and blew in, blotting out the sun. Rain that started slow pattered our skin to start. Fat drops turned heavy, then sharp and icy, turning her hair into a crystalline river of flickering copper and scarlet beneath the fast fading daylight.

"You want to get inside." I held out a hand as the wind picked up, pointing to the front of my cabin, and raised my straining voice to make myself heard over the deluge. "This is going to get torrential."

The woman standing in the middle of my yard stared at me through her ruined makeup. "I thought they were kidding about the rain." Her soft voice was whisked away by the wind.

Letting out a bark of a laugh that risked her wrath and probably some other version of fiery death, I grabbed her hand and towed her under the rafters of my cabin, out of the weather that seemed hell bent on giving her a fine mountain worthy greeting.

She squeaked, or made some sort of hyperactive noise that resembled a terrified animal as I pulled her close, but I only wanted to get that glorious hair out of her face. Unfortunately, my thick fingers weren't really up to the job. I smeared what was left of her makeup across her eyes until she resembled a trash panda wearing a damp party suit.

"You're not helping," she muttered, folding her arms across her chest. Her breasts pushed up. I tried not to stare.

"Probably not," I agreed, my lips twitching beneath my beard.

I sighed and shook my head. The ground shifted. I frowned, tightening my hold on the woman. She squeaked again when I pushed her back against the house, sure my luck had finally run out, but it wasn't me who the mountain took its wrath out on.

Movement in my periphery had me lunging sideways despite my better judgment, but nothing I did would have stopped the end result, anyway. Her little white car slid backward a foot. She moved with me even as I flung an arm across her chest, knocking her backward. The ground moved, and it was too late. The tiny car that matched the tiny woman lost its battle along with the topsoil remaining on my driveway under what was probably half a year's worth of rain in less than ten minutes since she arrived, if that.

The top of the hill collapsed, taking her car with it as she watched on in abject horror. A horrendous creak announced the vehicle's death as it slammed into what sounded like every granite boulder on its way to the bottom of the hill.

I waited until I thought it had fallen all the way down, then coughed into my fist.

"Well, that's that, then. Can I get you a coffee? I think I've got some UHT milk about in the pantry."

The horror reflected in her eyes probably matched my own, if for a slightly different reason. I wouldn't know. I didn't keep a mirror in the house, but she'd find that out soon enough.

Or a phone.

God knew who she'd been calling, but it sure as fuck hadn't been me.

I strode inside my home that had been built for one and now had to house two bodies. At least until I could figure out how the fuck to get her off my mountain and safely back to Red Hart before one of us killed the other.

Or worse.

CHAPTER THREE

FAITH

I stared around the small living area with its single, hand-hewn rocking chair, no television, zero tech, and what looked like a hand woven rug I suspected Walker had traded for maybe years ago from the track worn along one edge that seemed to match the width of his boots.

The whole lot overlooked a broad, open veranda where the rest of the mountain dropped away to one side, opposite to where I'd come in. His kitchen was there, too, small, built for one person, with a pantry as advertised, stocked to keep him alive for as long as he needed.

Seeing as he never left, that meant stocked well.

But the view from the rocker that looked out over the sheer cliff face beyond was what blew my mind. Mountains upon mountains spread out in glimpses between the falling sheets of rain that grayed the rest of my vision. Cold draughts blew into the log cabin he had built for himself in the ultimate version of rustic living in the literal middle of nowhere.

I wrapped my arms around myself as I watched the heavens open over us, shivering, but I couldn't tear my eyes away from the extreme vista with its brutal beauty laid out so bluntly right before me.

"It's different here. I know that." Walker stepped up behind me. His giant, oversized back shielded me from some of the wind that whipped around us. The pine and mountain scent of him filled my senses as I shook my head.

"No, it's not that. It's beautiful," I whispered, still staring through the rain. I had the impression that once it stopped and cleared I would be able to see for miles.

I hoped I would be here to see it when it did.

Then my reality crashed into me, and I squeezed my eyes shut, closing off the stunning view aid out before me. "My car." *My paperwork.* That had been on my car when it fell off the mountain.

"I'm sorry, Faith." A hesitant note entered Walker's voice before a large hand that matched the mountain man standing at my back cupped my shoulder. "It will be a while before we can leave and head down to...anywhere. I promised you coffee."

I bit my lip and nodded, willing the tears to stay at bay. "You did." Everything I'd had with me was in that car. My car that tipped off the edge of his mountain and sounded irrecoverable as it broke on every single solid surface on the way down. My bag containing my purse, my license and all my things in it. My coffee thermos and lunch that Eve had packed. The file with Walker Roan's notes in it.

Damnit, I'd wanted that thing off my desk, but this was not how I'd planned to achieve today's goals.

"Coffee would be lovely. Thank you."

Strange how, in the face of abject panic, we reverted to all the social niceties. Even from this wild man who had the sense to get me out of the pouring rain when my car fell off the edge of the world and into nothingness. For the first time it slammed into me why Travis and Jude had been so worried about me driving up here in the rain.

"Christ." I pressed a hand to my stomach, half

doubling over. "That could have been me in that car."

If I had taken a few minutes longer to reach him. If I had stayed inside, gathering my thoughts rather than jumping out to sass him, because I was sick of sitting on my ass.

If, if, if…

"It's okay, you potty mouthed thing." The hand on my shoulder patted me awkwardly. "How do you take it?"

Rough, fast and with a side of mountain man freshness.

I turned and blinked at him, my reply ready to go because no landslide was going to steal my options today. I blinked when I found deep brown eyes staring at me edged with concern.

"Ah, take what?" Maybe my response needed to be limited, given the circumstances.

His beard twitched, and I wanted to run my fingers through it.

"Coffee, Faith. How do you take your coffee?"

"Black, please. Sugar if you have it. None if you don't. I'm not fussy."

His beard twitched again. "So it seems."

I didn't know what to make of that cryptic comment, so I followed him away from the stunning vista and into the small kitchen where he planted me on one side of the short bench on a single stool while he headed into the walk around pantry at the back.

"You made this place yourself, didn't you?"

"With the help of Travis and Jude, the summer that Jude first turned up at Red Hart. The year—"

"Your father kicked you out," I finished for him softly.

Walker reappeared with a large tin of powdered coffee that didn't actually dwarf his hands. His lips, even beneath his beard, seemed set in a tight line. "That's right. You know my history as well as I do, don't you?"

I swallowed hard. "It's a good thing that everything I had with me that fell off the side of your mountain is also backed up on this." I extracted my phone out of my pocket and waved it at him.

He eyed the device like he might snatch it from my hand and toss it off the cliff face himself. "Better shut that off," he said abruptly.

"Why, because you don't want to face your past?" I raised an eyebrow.

Instantly, I felt shitty that I'd come back with a snap when here he was trying to make me feel better. I wouldn't even be in this situation, invading his space and stuck if I hadn't done what the Red Hart boys recommended in the first place and stayed at the bottom of his mountain.

Not that I'd admit to that.

Walker watched me for a long, silent moment. Finally, he shook his head. "There's no reception here, Faith. If you leave that on, it'll be flat in a few hours. I don't have a charger for anything new and I don't imagine you have one stuffed into those skin tight pants."

His gaze drifted over my body, what he could see of me tucked away behind the bench, then jerked his attention back to my face.

My mouth hung open. "Oh." Was Mister *I-don't-do-people-on-my-mountain* just checking me out?

A second sneaky look back at his face caught his gaze coasting over mine and settling on my lips. *He was.* Game changer. Now I knew where we stood. I could play by those rules, because Walker Roan was a different kind of eye candy, but he was eye candy, nonetheless. And he wasn't my client, so I wasn't breaking any rules...yet.

I frowned, trying to figure out what we had been talking about before we dropped into accidental flirt mode because that was safer and I wasn't ready for this...not quite yet. My mind needed caffeine to activate, apparently. I recounted what I knew about Red Hart's history.

"Jude and Travis must have been young." Jude had his own stories to tell.

"They were. Fifteen. Too much energy, randy, gangly as hell, about ten years younger than me. But I needed the assist, and they needed direction for a summer. Just not from Trav's Pa back then, rest his soul."

I bit my lip and nodded. Red Hart's land was laced with its own tragedy.

Walker stopped talking, his voice dry and raspy. He coughed more than once as he made coffee for us both and pushed one large, chipped mug across to me. I ran my fingers across the rough clay surface, then looked down at the rug.

"These are all local, traded things. Aren't they?" I looked back at him.

Walker shrugged, as if to say *what of it?* He seemed to be done talking for the time being. He ran his hand across the edge of the thick wood benchtop where his arms rested, and I recalled the wood he'd been chopping when I arrived earlier. Maybe he traded heavy hand crafts with Kyle, or did custom jobs. Those paid well, and he seemed to have decent skill with wood.

I risked another glance at him, but Walker was definitely done talking for now. I didn't blame him in the least. I'd invaded his home, stayed longer by far already than I ever intended, and I hadn't even broached the topic I was supposed to be talking about.

I did, however, take his advice, and turn off my phone. If he thought my device would be flat in a few hours without charge, then I'd be here for much longer. Which begged the question...how much longer? A quick glance outside showed thick gray clouds with no sign of the rain abating.

"It'll be a while, huh?" I looked back at Walker when he didn't talk.

He just watched me and when I stared at him, my panic rising, he reached across and pressed my mug into my hands.

I looked down at my forgotten black coffee, surprised. Grateful for the distraction, I picked up the cup of cheap black ambrosia and took a sip. Sweet, thick liquid scalded my throat. I took another, using the quick burst of pain to ease my panic until a rumble from across the bench indicated Walker's approval.

"Thank you," I whispered, more than a little horrified when tears stung my eyes. I blinked rapidly, looking out at the rain instead. It wasn't like I should be looking anywhere else. Certainly not at the tattooed, wild man behemoth who saw way too much right now. "Is the house likely to follow my car on its slide down the mountain? At least it would make it a quick trip back to the big house at Red Hart," I said lightly.

Walker rumbled again, a noise I took for his laughter. "No," he said quietly. I thought he was finished talking, but then he surprised me, reaching across the benchtop to close work calloused hands over mine where they clasped my mug. "You're safe here, Faith."

With me.

He didn't say it, but then, he didn't need to. After that, we drank coffee in his kitchen while the rain poured down and didn't talk at all.

And my panic never returned.

Walker Roan's cabin contained exactly six rooms which was three more than I expected: A living area, a kitchen, plus pantry, which I counted as one space. His bedroom, his bathroom, and a spare room right across the short hall from where he slept.

That was where he left me when the light faded for good for the night, and he set a fire in the living area, sitting quietly in his rocker as he stared pensively into the flames. Unwilling to disturb Walker's quiet mindset that seemed to be his normal, I sat on the veranda hardwood floor a few feet away from him. My arms wrapped around my knees as I watched the rain that showed no sign of letting up, much in the same manner as he did the fire.

And the silence, interspersed with its white noise that seemed held at a distance by the darkness that didn't dare to enter his space while he was inside it, and constant crackles from the fireplace, wasn't deafening or uncomfortable at all.

Somehow, with Walker Roan at my back, our combined arm's reach distance away from each other, I wasn't half as scared as I thought I might be in this place. A world away from anything where he was a kind of mountain god, perched in this place so far from everyone and everything by choice.

When the night air grew cold and my light shivers stopped, my arms numbing, he seemed to notice my discomfort, or lack thereof. A heavy blanket that smelled of sharp spruce and spicy male and leather scents dropped around my shoulders. His hands pressed down, then lifted me up.

I gasped at the ease he lifted me in his arms, sweeping the blanket beneath me so his arms never contacted bare skin. Suddenly I was looking at the inside of his beard, my cheek resting over the vicinity of his heart, through the thick weave of the blanket that broke the space between us.

I frowned, butting my cheek against his covered shoulder until he coughed a laugh.

"Are you right there, Precious?" Dark eyes watched me, reflecting starlight the rain obscured.

I blinked up, white noise blocking out everything else but him. "What, are you giving me a stripper name, now?"

"Do you need one?" He raised an eyebrow. "Let's get you to bed." My breath hitched. He sighed. "Your bed, Presh. Not mine."

"Such a disappointment."

My feet hit the floor. I scrabbled for a moment as pins and needles shot up my legs after having them folded for so long. His arm gripped mine—through the blanket, of course. I clung to the offensive but warm piece around me.

"Thank you for offering me your place and not sending me off down the hill." I tried to recover.

"I wouldn't do that." He looked affronted even as his voice strained. A hand raked through his beard. "Come on. I won't sleep if you're wandering about the place on your own tonight."

"Just tonight?" I closed my mouth with a snap when he shot me a sharp glance. "Sorry. I'm not used to watching what I have to say," I apologized.

"You shouldn't have to," he said gruffly. "A woman should speak her mind."

I stared at his back. "You're the only one of your species who thinks that," I said softly.

Walker didn't stop moving in his retreat along the hallway toward the bedrooms, but his shoulders did flex beneath his chequered shirt, so I knew he heard me. He didn't stop walking until he reached the spare room that I guessed I would be calling home until the rain stopped and either we went down the mountain or Jude and Travis made it up somehow to collect me.

I still winced internally that I'd gone against their suggestions and hadn't listened, but I was here now, and the damage had been done. I'd wear their combined glowers when I returned to ground level, whenever that happened. Eventually. I just had to survive until then, in the company of a somewhat grumpy mountain man, and try not to let my outspoken lawyer ass impeach on his space too much.

"I can help out around the place a bit," I blurted as he began to turn back to me. "I can sew, a bit, if you need stuff fixed. And I can cook. If you need legal things done while I'm here, apart from what I came up here to do—" I wasn't letting him off the hook *that* damn easily. "—then I can work on that, too. I have a full business back at White Cap and if you do have other internet connectivity or tech, then I'll log in through that. I work my own accounts—"

"You don't have to pay your way, Faith. I'm happy to have you here." A muscle flexing in his jaw beneath the edge of his beard smattered where the deep brown smattered with a few red and silver hairs told the truth of his lie.

I swallowed. "Okay," I whispered, not knowing where to go from there.

He nodded. "This is you. Take the blanket with you. It gets cold. There's my spare clothes in the drawers. They'll be too big for you, but you can sleep in them until we clean yours, alright?"

Tears stung the back of my eyes at his kindness, but I refused to let them fall before this mountain of a man who let me into his home without a single objection so far.

"Thank you. I'm sorry..." I bit my lip. He had said not to apologize. "Thank you," I repeated again, and turned into the bedroom lit with its lamp. The light flickered as I crossed the threshold and went out.

I froze in place, my breaths coming short as pitch darkness encompassed me. Suddenly the rain sounded louder, and the wind seemed to rock the log cabin in its place where it became all too obvious that we were perched on the edge of the mountain. I wanted nothing more than to run back to the false protection of the fireplace in Walker's all too exposed living area and huddle before the open flames and their faux protection.

Or turn and hide the behemoth's arms at my back. Either round of security would do just fine.

"Fuck," Walker cursed softly at my back. "The sun's gone. Solar power's run out for the night. We didn't have a lot of sunlight today. I'll fill the jenny up and give you more light."

My brain kicked into gear. "The generator isn't near the house, is it?"

I didn't recall seeing anything on this side when I arrived earlier, though I'd only had a snapshot of his rustic living area before the clouds swept around the mountainside that appeared to have been hiding from me for my three hour crawl across Red Hart land and up Walker's mountain.

"No, it's around the other side, near the shed." His finger trailed across my temple. I nearly jumped at the contract, then relaxed as I realized he offered me comfort with the touch, leaning into his hand. He stilled, but didn't pull away.

"Don't go out there. It's only darkness. The weather is filthy. I'll survive." I kept my voice light like the lights going out was no big deal.

Utter bullshit. The moment he left I would be lucky I didn't climb on the bed and run in circles, screaming my lungs out like a three year old. At least, in my head.

Lie. I'd absolutely be under the covers, screaming silently into my cupped hands until my breath ran out to the memory of my car sliding off the side of the hill and hitting everything on the way down, wondering if the house would be the next to fall into oblivion taking us with it.

It's survived for at least fifteen years up here. It will survive one more night.

And the next that I stayed here. And the one after that.

However long I had to remain in Walker Roan's home. Away from everyone and everything.

He never did answer that question on tech. Had I asked one? Or just blundered in with an offer, as per usual, and hoped he would deluge me with information? I got the impression that Walker wasn't the free information sharing type of guy.

Jude and Travis had spoiled me for country cowboys forever. But Walker Roan wasn't a cowboy, was he? He was a mountain man personified, and he would be lucky, I guessed, to see one or two people a season, if not in a whole year. His social circle probably included a few squirrels, the Red Hart boys and a bear or two.

"Bears. You have a whole wall missing. One entire side of your *house* is open. How do you keep out wild animals?" I turned on my heel and gaped at him.

Not that I could see his face, but the touch of his hand didn't drop away, curving around my cheek instead. The touch was intimate, warm and grounding. His fingers were rough and calloused, his palm gentle and oversized where he cupped my face.

Walker could crush me all too easily, I knew with strength like his, muscle popping out everywhere and not the useless gym based city sort. His was the real deal, work hardened.

But he stepped into me, I knew by the increased

warmth of him alone. My hands rose to press against his chest or his stomach, discovering hard planes of muscle I suspected wore as much ink as the trails that decorated his neck and forearms.

"Cliff face, remember? The house is built right to the edge. Jude, Trav and I designed it that way. The squirrels can get in. Maybe a few rodents, though they don't bother me. Once a snake, but it ended up as my dinner that night." I could hear the smile in his voice as I let out the shudder he intended me to give, and he laughed softly, drawing me a little closer.

I didn't object.

"No bears or wolves?" I didn't want to share my bed with that sort of carnivore. A different type, maybe...

"None, Faith," Walker reassured me, his voice deepening. "You're safe here. I promise."

I nodded into his touch, letting my eyes drift shut as I rested my cheek into his palm.

His breath stalled as I gave him my trust willingly. A second later he leaned down, and his lips brushed my temple. "Sleep," he whispered, pulling my blanket tight around my shoulders. "I'm right here if you need me."

Then he was gone, and I stood alone in my doorway. The only light I could see was the faint reflected flicker from the fire further along the hallway that showed my own personal bear of a man disappearing into the room straight across from me. Walker hesitated before his door closed, not quite all the way. From the noise outside, the storm has resumed as my company for the night.

But I wasn't afraid of what I couldn't see in the dark anymore.

CHAPTER FOUR

WALKER

My new housemate was a dancer as well as a lawyer —a hurdle I knew she wouldn't let me dodge, though for now I satisfied myself in watching her hips bounce around inside my borrowed clothes.

Faith danced when she made the bed in my spare room. I knew, because she hadn't shut the door the night before. I swore my old Army sweats never looked so good, even with the cuffs rolled up a half dozen times.

She danced in the kitchen too, a reduced version of what she did in the bedroom, bopping her hips about as she drank her first coffee of the day. The rate she imbibed that stuff gave me the impression

I'd need to get her down to Red Hart sooner than I expected or she'd drink me dry.

Not too soon, because something about having Faith Somerset in my home reminded me of what it was like to share my space with another person for more than a few scant hours.

And...I liked it.

Having her around. Loud, crass, and filthy mouthed. Faith already made me question the way I set myself up, the choices I'd made over the years. As uncomfortable as that made me in the first few hours we shared the same breathing air while the rain thundered down on my roof, I also liked that she challenged me.

It had been a whole lot of years since anyone had the balls to do that, probably longer to my face.

"When do we start?" I winced at the words that left my mouth, but she'd come here to do a job, and now she was stuck in a place that didn't suit her.

The least I could do was give her the courtesy of my attention before I turned her down.

Besides, it gave me a reason to look at her wherever she talked, and by God could that woman use her mouth. Which made me wonder, while her hips swayed gently and the rain kept her locked away inside my house, what else she might use her pretty, cherry lips for.

Then I banished those thoughts and tried to look civilized while she turned those color change eyes on me, lit with enough hope that my room felt like the sun rose and the rain stopped.

I checked over her shoulder before I dashed her hopes past a month of Sundays.

It hadn't. Rain still lashed the side of the mountain in sheets, some of the spray entering the veranda as a gust of wind caught it and lifted the icy droplets to cover her feet.

"Come away. You'll end up freezing, or sick." I planted her ass in my chair and leaned against the wall instead. "Tell me what you came up here to say."

Faith studied the bottom of her coffee mug and said nothing.

My eyebrows rose as the silence stretched out. "What?" I prompted her. "Surely my father didn't frighten you so badly that you can't tell me what he wanted you to say without all your pieces of paper or your phone on?" All the papers that disappeared down the mountain along with her car. Guilt assuaged me as my voice ran out of juice at that point.

I folded my arms over my chest and refused flat out to cough, though my throat itched mother-fucking abominably. I was done talking. Now it was her turn.

She peeked up at me through her lashes. I had no idea if Faith knew just how cute she looked, stuffed into my oversized clothing that hung off her tiny frame, her flame colored hair tousled about her like I'd fucked her seven ways from Friday, but she bit her lip and doubled the effect in seconds. "Can I invade your pantry and make my own coffee this time? Pretty please?" Her bare feet, still slightly damp, dangled off the edge of my hand made rocker that I broke twenty times just in the process of designing the thing. She sank deep into the pillows that supported my back like I'd carved it just for her.

I swallowed hard and jerked my head to one side. "Yeah. Did I fu– didn't I make it right?"

She shrugged and struggled to get off the edge, like Goldilocks trying to get out of Papa Bear's too-big chair. "Could be a bit stronger."

I bit back a laugh. "Stronger? Girl, I emptied half the tin into that thing."

She grinned back at me, swinging her feet off the edge of my seat. "Mmm. Might be able to teach you a thing or two yet."

Shaking my head, I reached down and slid my hands under her arms and lifted her along my front, taking the few steps to my kitchen and placed her on the granite stone floor. Her toes touched the cold ground. She squeaked, looking down, then back at me with wide eyes.

It didn't take long for her to track the marks carved deep into the stone that took the Red Hart teens—then—and me the better part of two years to carve out once the boys left me alone.

"You built the house in the literal mountain?" she whispered.

I swore if her eyes got any wider, she'd pop out of existence and turn into an anime princess. The girl was a walking wet dream. I rubbed the back of my neck.

"Yeah." I cleared my throat. "Want a tour of what's back there?"

I'd only needed to make her a basic dinner of ramen noodles and stock soup plus coffee the night before and this morning, plus some toast so I hadn't needed to go far, which was probably how she came to the conclusion that's all the pantry did.

My comment seemed to hit home. Her mouth opened then shut and she nodded once. Fast.

I held out my hand. *Mistake.* But I did it anyway.

She wound her fingers around mine, her touch soft and warm, like it had been when she rested her face against my palm last night. That had been a mistake, too, because it had been a damn close thing, wanting to invite her into my bed instead of leaving her to sleep in hers.

And sleep she did, purring away with the sort of resonation that meant that while she got rest, I did not. Not that I minded. If she slept, she felt safe, and that had been the goal.

Yeah, fucking right.

I ignored the pulse of arousal that half-hardened my dick on sight and turned my back to her, taking a too-large step that towed her along behind me.

"Sorry."

My next step was a touch shorter as I turned the corner beside the fridge that thankfully kept everything cold until this morning when I walked out into the rain and poured fuel into the jenny anyway, well before she woke up. It had been my mistake in letting it run down the week before.

"It's okay. Thank you for showing me around. This is—" Her words and breath hitched, both, and she stopped talking for a moment. "Fucking amazing," Faith breathed at my back.

Light fingertips pressed into my spine on either

side of my spine as I stopped in the middle of the small row that traveled long into the mountain side that turned a sort of corner.

So did my house.

The outside kept along the flat rock. That's where the bedrooms were, where we slept the night before. Hers bordered onto the rock face at the back, which was why it got cold in there. Not because of the exposure to wind, but because the rock itself seemed to leech a sense of coldness into the room beyond the plaster Jude insisted I use rather than leaving the bald rock as the wall like I'd wanted.

In case someone ever visited, apart from him.

Like who? I'd asked back then. He'd sent me a knowing glance, and I nearly cuffed the kid who'd grown up to become one of my closest—and only—friends.

Having Faith in my space now and giving her a tour hadn't seemed like a really shitty idea—until this moment. Her tiny hands pressed insistently to my spine, flattening against my back. My muscles tightened beneath my shirt, I stiffened in place.

"What are you doing?"

She shifted and shoved and woman-handled me until her tight body slid right around mine—her hands wrapping right around my waist somehow in their own personal discovery orbit—until she stood at my front instead of at my back.

"You are a big boy, aren't you, Walker Roan? Wow. That was a journey. Now, you can't tell a girl there's coffee and a secret cave in your house, and then stand between her and both of those things, can you?"

My lips twitched. "I suppose not."

It had been so long since I interacted with a woman—and certainly never a woman like Faith Somerset—that I'd forgotten what flirting felt like. It wasn't like I didn't sort out my own physical needs when they hit me. I was a man like any other, and I took care of the urges as they came on. But having her in my space, so close, so tiny and soft and goddam tempting, smelling like my own damn soap and shampoo like I'd personally branded her and she had let me when she showered and used my shit last night—that was a different sort of torture.

One I liked way too fucking much.

She's not staying. She can't and she won't if I ask her to stay.

And she'll annoy the shit out of me after more than a day.

I knew that last would be the truth. It was one of the reasons I left everyone else to their own devices

—quite literally—and the world, and discovered my own personal slice of it. Plus, from what she'd told me earlier Faith had her own little setup down the mountain. She'd never leave that for a man like me.

My heart panged at the thought. An organ I long forgot resided within me. Hell, I didn't even know how old she was. Thirty, maybe? That had to make her ten years or so younger than me.

She nodded decisively. "Good, then."

Her tone caught me off guard. "Good, what?"

"I'll go wandering. There's no bears back here, right? Or traps?"

I smirked. "Don't fall in the pool."

"The what?"

I leaned against the shelving that held my beer and waited. Her footsteps, already light as she padded barefoot away from me, grew faint. I counted in my head, then my brow furrowed as nothing came back at me. Wait. Maybe she had fallen in. What if—

"Faith?" I started forward, pushing myself off the shelfs with a burst of breath as my chest tightened at the thought of something happening to her on my mountain. The vision of yesterday, her car that could have had her in it tumbling backward as I grabbed for her though she'd never been in any danger, thank Christ, strangled my heart. "Presh, tell me you—"

"Holy fuck, big boy. You have been holding out on me." Her voice echoed weirdly along the tunnel that I'd dug all the way to the hot/cold springs that gave me a source of freshwater as well as a therapeutic spa bath.

Coach lanterns I'd rigged up on wires kept the light dim but the tunnel usable.

"Don't drink it, small town girl," I warned as she dangled her toes in the hot pool, ignoring the cold ones where my taps ran from on the right, and a deeper one I used to wake myself up with occasionally. "That one is purely for bathing in."

"Yeah, I figured that out, but thanks." She lowered her ankle into the water and gasped. "Okay, I am coming back here tonight." She glanced back at me, sucking her lower lip between her teeth the way she seemed to do when she was unsure of something. "Is it safe?"

"If I said no would you do it anyway?" I whisked that safety net she thought I provided away just to see what she'd do.

"Probably. This is too tempting." Faith dragged her foot out, and swirled her fingers through the water. "How did you find this?"

I shrugged. "Trav's dad, Len, knew this was up here. They owned the land for a long time, knew all its secrets. He sold me a patch under the provision that I wouldn't change too much or cut off the river that flowed through his land. So, we worked around it."

"It's a good change." She nodded. "Do you use it?"

"A lot of nights after I've worked my ass off. It helps–" I cut my words off.

She looked at me. "What hurts, bear boy?"

"Nothing."

A snort erupted from her. "You're so full of shit."

"Potty mouth, Precious. Such a potty mouth."

"You are talking a lot today." She smiled prettily as my mouth snapped shut on demand. Blazing red hair flickered out behind her as she sauntered past me.

And all my broken brain could picture was her in the hot water without a stitch on, her hair drifting around her, and my clothes tossed somewhere behind her on the granite.

Shaking my head to clear the vision that did nobody any good, I braced my hands over my head against the cold stone, feeling the weight of the mountain bear down on me. "Come on, Precious.

Let's get you that coffee. Don't you have a story to tell?"

Faith tossed me a sassy grin over her shoulder like she knew exactly what was on my mind. All the way back into my cabin, I swore her hips swayed a little more.

CHAPTER FIVE

FAITH

Walker Roan was a stubborn man. Plus, his tech was at least a decade out of date, and that didn't help with anything. I did manage to pull up his father's will before the internet died for good. I knew he had to have read that, though from the look on his face when I glanced across at him it hadn't been any time recently, and he may not have read it all the way through to the end.

"Didn't anyone go through this with you at the time?" I asked gently.

His beard shifted side to side, which I took as a *no*.

"Okay. Welp. He wanted you to take on the land he left behind."

"No."

I sucked in a long breath. We had been over this a dozen times already. Walker listened politely, gave me all his attention and when we got to this point, his answer was the same each time.

No.

No

No.

Fucking *No.*

No wonder he never got to the end of the document. I guessed his answer had been the same back then. I also guessed that at some point he got up and left the meeting, and that was when the papers were delivered to me the next day.

That meeting should have been mine, but at the time the firm I worked for decided that one of the partners should handle it because they knew better.

Also *no.*

I licked my lips. "Do you understand what will happen to the land if you don't come to collect on it?"

He nodded. "Yep."

"And you don't care?" I kept my tone carefully neutral. Because even though Walker was stubborn and I'd been in his house for around twenty-four hours, I'd grown to care for him. I'd spent far more years looking after his father, but I could see the resemblances between them both.

Also, I loved that piece of land. I'd driven past it many times over the years on the way into white cap, back when I was studying, on my way home. I had to, and it kind of heralded my return that I was back *home*.

Okay, so I was invested. And maybe there was a good reason why I hadn't been reading that day. But also someone who cared about the family should have maybe negotiated with this man and not left him bereft of his inheritance then so we weren't at this pivotal point now.

And I still wanted to scream at him about it, but I didn't.

Don't you care about your father's legacy? That it will be chopped up and parceled out into roads and other developments around White Cap?

I closed my eyes and breathed through my nose. "You'd only have to come off the mountain once. Just set foot on the land. Claim it is yours. I'll look after the taxes. You can keep it for—"

"What, my grandchildren?"

I raised my eyebrows encouragingly at the first alternative to 'no' I'd heard in the last hour.

Walker snorted. "Because I see so many opportunities for those around here."

"Well, if you got off the mountain, maybe you would have a chance to make some," I said tartly.

Walker leaned across the small fold out table where he had placed his ancient laptop that miraculously booted up with the help of three hours of long overdue updates, and placed his scarred, inked hands on my wrists.

"Faith, listen to me. My answer is no," he said softly.

I bit my lip, staring into his liquid brown eyes and hated that I was about to do this.

Because there was no way I left town and drove all the way up his mountain without a trump card in my back pocket.

"Even if the reason the land is being taken away from you under a stack of clauses isn't for roads, Walker? It's because the roads are being built to put a casino into White Cap."

His hands tightened on my wrists. "What?"

A zing of tension rocketed between us as his eyes flashed.

I knew I had him. I just hated that I'd had to do

it. Paul Roan spent his life protesting and fighting again putting poker machines in the local bars in White Cap. Then the advent of a prospective casino. He spearheaded a massive campaign that prevented the plans for years. Most of my teen and college semesters were spent checking in on him while he made sure that the casino never went ahead, claiming the jobs created wouldn't be the sort that the town needed. Walker had already left by then.

Then he got old, and sick. But he had spurred the town into action, and the campaigns continued well after he and Walker fell out.

Now Paul Roan was gone and the legacy he left behind was about to be divvied up by corrupt politicians I couldn't prevent from doing what they wanted, lining their pockets with the sale of his land.

But Walker could. *If* he could move his ass down his mountain in the next two months, and decided to keep that land. Do something with it. Which meant he needed to come off the mountain more often.

And that was the crux of his 'no'...until right now.

"Faith?" he asked, a warning in his voice.

I didn't want to, but...needs must. Today fell under that caveat.

"I knew your father well, Walker. Really well." It was my voice that strained this time, instead of his. "I don't know if you remember, but I was at his funeral. I was the one hiding in the back because I couldn't face anyone that day. I handled his legal accounts for years."

Walker frowned. "You weren't at the will reading, I would have remembered you." His eyes never flinched from mine as he made that declaration.

Something lanced straight through my chest, like his gaze passed right through me. His thumbs brushed the backs of my hands where he hadn't let me go, and his fingers shifted to close around mine.

"No. They—I wasn't allowed to be present. Too distraught, or something." I hiccupped at the memory.

"Fucking assholes," he growled, reaching out to sweep my hair back from my face. When the strand just kept going and going he curled it around one fist until he reached the end and tugged gently. "Just because someone cares about another human does not mean they are inept."

I blinked at him through stinging eyes. "For a man who refuses to see other humans and didn't talk to his father for the better part of ten years, you have a remarkable sense of what they are about," I whispered.

Walker started. His hands opened, freeing mine. My hair unraveled from his fist and fell back to my lap. "My answer is still no."

He pushed away from the small table, closed the laptop with a snap, and shifted the outdated tech away from me without a second glance.

"Fucking mountain man," I grumbled as I sank into the hot water in his cave pool, bitching all the while. "Stupid, stubborn man and his stupid, stubborn mountain." I splashed a bit just because I could, and stamping my feet did sweet fuck all in the water.

I mean, stomping bedrock wasn't satisfying in the least, certainly not when there was no one else around to see me do it.

"Are you always this vocal when you whine about other people, or should I get out and leave you to it?" Walker's voice emanated from the other pool.

The cold pool.

"What the fuck are you doing over there?" I shrieked, submerging way too fast in the hot water and upping my temperature at a speed my body did not cope well with.

My hair tangled in the water around me, swirling in tiny eddies like a noose until I wrapped myself up in red tentacles that also happened to be attached to my head. Wet hair was horribly heavy. I knew I should have knotted it on top of my head, but the idea of it swirling around me seemed romantic...until right now.

I fought my way out of my cocoon with the grace of a waterlogged hippo and flung my hair at a rock to free myself of its grip.

"I'm bathing," came the calm reply, seemingly through a wall of rock, though I knew there were air pockets between the pools because I'd spotted them when I did my little discovery tour earlier in the week when Walker first let me into his secret man cave shit.

Almost a whole week. That's how long I'd been in his home. I was no closer to succeeding in negotiations with him. My phone was totally flat, I had no reception before that and as far as I could tell, Jude and Travis would only know that I was stuck on the mountain by the fact I never returned like I promised.

I hoped they figured that out and didn't just think I'd gone back to White Cap.

Because as great a host as Walker Roan was, I still needed to return to my own life, my business and my clients. Even though we hadn't killed each other just yet, it had been a close thing a few times.

Plus, it was still raining. Which was why I had finally succumbed to the temptations of the underground hot pool. Otherwise, I froze my ass off in the log cabin cave that, although pretty, also wasn't home. Though with Walker nearby, it was sorta starting to feel like it, staring out at the gray skies. A big part of me wanted to see what was beyond.

Another part of me wanted the sky to stay that way and never change because...

That meant not having to go back.

Not for the first time I'd sat there looking at the rain I couldn't see beyond while Walker stared into the fire from his chair. I wondered what it would be like to just...stop.

To not go back. Not to have clients and responsibilities. Not to have a business. Just to shut up shop and...exist.

Like Walker Roan did.

Then my brain kicked in, told me that was the stuff of impossible dreams, and my planning went on and on and on again. I forced my mind back to the situation at hand, because the idea of staying here with Walker was far too...romantic.

I didn't want to have those sorts of thoughts about anyone.

"Why are you in the cold pool?" I frowned. "I thought you were having a shower?"

"I did."

"But you didn't follow me down here."

"There's more than one entry into this part of the mountain, Precious." I could freaking *hear* the smirk in his voice.

"Asshole," I muttered and leaned back into the water that muted whatever he said next. "Sorry, I can't hear you," I singsonged, just to be a brat, because I was feeling the vibe.

The water rippled around me and something splashed my face. A large something.

I sprang up, lurching half out of the water. "What—"

"The water got too cold." Walker blinked innocently at me, but my mountain man had never been innocent, not once in his damn life.

Plus, I just gave him an eyeful from the waist up, naked tits and all, when I threw myself out of the water thinking a bear got in with me.

Because a bear did get into the hot pool with me.

I wrapped my hair around me like a cocoon a second time, but at least now it was by design. "I thought you were supposed to do it the other way around," I grumped as he watched me with curious eyes. "Hot pool, then cold pool."

Walker shrugged. "I've never been worried about others' expectations." He caught one loose end of my hair and held the wavering end in his large, scarred hand in the water. "What happens if I pull on this?"

I stared at him breathlessly. "Do it, and see."

His mouth flickered at once side, his eyes dark pools on their own in the flickering light that reflected off the water's rippling source. He wrapped the strand of my hair around his finger, tugging once as he moved closer until I could see the fine smattering of hair that covered his chest. Inked, as I suspected, all the way across his shoulders and chest and down to his stomach. That one tug was all he did, and he then let go.

Disappointment merged with a hot rush of need that the pool swept away. We stared at each other across a small expanse of unbroken water, then he turned away and swam across the pool with long, sure strokes until he reached the far wall.

And stayed there.

"You're safe here, Faith. I promise." His raspy voice, ruined from talking so much with me after what seemed to be years of not speaking to anyone at all apart from what was probably a handful of squirrels or other assorted wildlife, gave out to a faint whisper.

But I still heard him.

I sank lower in the water, pretending the heat I shared from his mountain came from him instead and gave him my equally soft answer.

"I know."

CHAPTER SIX

WALKER

Faith occupied my spare room for a week. I managed to keep my hands off her while it rained, but it was a near thing. Her presence occupied my every waking thought. The night before in the pool, when she flung her body out of the water, I got to see just how perfect she was.

Not skin and bones, but perfectly toned all over, perfectly in proportion. She wasn't too small or too big. Just...her. Faith. I'd be damned if I didn't want to call her mine. Make her mine, here, on my mountain, where I wanted her to stay and never let her go.

It was impossible.

I kept my hands and my opinions to myself,

waiting across the pool with my gaze averted until she was out of the water and wrapped in a towel before I let my eyes wander back to her bare feet that had become something of an obsession for me.

I hadn't lied to her when I said that the wall adjoining the warm/cold pool room beneath the mountain also had a walk around wall that led to my shower. The whole thing was like a circle. I could collect a beer from the pantry without leaving my bedroom, technically.

I showered cold the next morning, and headed out to the kitchen hoping the rain had cleared so I could see what damage had been done and what I could fix from here. Not that there would be much I could do; we'd either be walking down to the ranch or the boys would be driving up to collect her at some point. My bet was on the former.

My secondary bet with myself was that Faith and her high heels wouldn't like that idea much at all.

I paused at her doorway that sat a few inches ajar telling myself I was just checking in on her, making sure she was alright this morning. Which was true—but ever since the first morning I'd seen her dance, that, along with her bare feet, had become my newest obsession.

Today was no exception, and she didn't disappoint.

Because Faith had decided that today, she had forgone clothes.

Not altogether, just mine. The borrowed component. She still wore the lace underwear she washed fastidiously and managed to dry—partially because there wasn't much of it. Her luscious as fuck breasts were cupped in scalloped gold lace that matched the semitransparent panties that hugged her ass like a second skin.

Some of the lace disappeared between her rounded ass cheeks as she bent forward, folding her body in half and I suppressed a groan. I wanted to trace my fingers along the backs of her thighs, feel her heat and earn her moans as I touched her while she danced for me, swaying and arching like she did now, her ass pressed backward to the bed.

Fuck.

I raked my nails over my scalp, using the pain to bring myself back. She didn't need a randy hermit of a man lusting after her when all she probably wanted was to get out of my damn hair—what was left of it. I didn't agree with what she wanted from me, what she hauled her stunning ass all the way up here to do.

The least I could provide was a safe space where I didn't perv on her like some motherfucking creeper.

Growling under my breath, I stormed along the corridor to the kitchen, determined to find her a giant coffee mug and make her the biggest, hottest and strongest drink I could for the morning.

I'd barely set myself to my task for a handful of minutes when she clattered her way into my space, joining me along the bench instead of the other side of it.

"Morning, grumpy," she said, way too cheerful.

I looked down at her, sweating one of my long sleeved tops—and what looked like nothing else. Well, nothing else, because creeper me knew exactly what she had on under the soft, oversized material that hung to her knees anyway, but she'd forgotten something critical this morning.

"The hell are you doing, Presh?" I pushed the half-made coffee in her direction and stepped back.

It still wasn't enough space as she reached around me to snag the room temperature, heat treated milk.

"Making coffee. Maybe toast. Do you want anything?" She made herself busy as usual and lived up to the promise she had tried to make to me on that first day back when I'd been an utter asshole and shut her down for offering.

I cringed at the memory as she pirouetted past me, the hem of my shirt riding up along her thighs to give me more than a glimpse of creamy, curved flesh the perfect shape for my palm.

Palms that itched to see how her body fit against the shape of my hands.

"Did you forget something important when you left the bedroom?" I bit my tongue on saying more.

The woman before me had me saying more words than I'd managed in over fifteen years. I still haven't worked out if that was a good or a bad thing.

"Like that?" She pirouetted back in the opposite direction, giving me a glimpse of her other thigh.

The view matched.

"Like pants, Faith."

She laughed at me, and flipped the hem up in full to flash me her lace panties that just covered her ass. I'd already seen that view, but close up she was even more tantalizing than before. "Nah. I got sick of rolling the legs up every ten seconds when they fell down. Decided this was long enough. Right?" Her eyes were full of mischief and something else I couldn't quite interpret.

I snarled, grabbing the material out of her hand and yanked it back down. "Don't do that."

"What?" She gaped at me. "Are you a eunuch as well as a hermit? I mean, I didn't check last night, but—"

All sense left me. I grabbed her waist and pinned her back against the bench, screwing the thought of making sure she had space and wasn't terrified of me overwhelming her. Her lips fell into a perfect 'o' shape as I ground my very much *not* eunuch-y hardness against her stomach.

"No, Faith. It's not that I don't want you," I grated, my voice deciding now was the perfect time to give up for the day already, fuck it. "I'm just fucking terrified what it means if I do push my luck with you. Because I've still got to get you safely down the mountain and that's gonna be real fucking hard to do if I screw up the trust we've garnered between us into next week. You feel me?" I braced my arms behind her, leaning into her space so she had to arch backwards just to look up at me, or continue breathing.

Not that I really gave her a choice, because for just one moment, I did want her to feel me. All of me. And I wanted her to make that choice so damn bad, I ached for her.

Then sense slammed into me and I dropped my hands, retreating fast.

"Fuck. I'm sorry. I shouldn't have touched you."

Silence fell in my kitchen as she panted. Her whole body trembled as she straightened, her hair tangled over my bench like some crazy red-headed Rapunzel variation.

Faith shook her head. "I know you've been watching me."

I blinked at her. My mouth dried. "What?"

"Last night, in the pool when you backed off. If you'd stayed I...wouldn't have objected. I mean..." Her cheeks flushed. "I didn't mean to flash you with a full frontal, but I wouldn't have objected."

"I tried not to look." *I am so full of shit.* She was utterly glorious. "I didn't want to scare you."

"I know."

My chest rose on fast, long breaths. "I'm sorry, Faith." I shook my head. "This is my fault. I've been trying not to be attracted to you all damn week. This is why I shouldn't be near people. Why I left—"

"Bullshit." She shot me a fiery glare that would have asked a city boy. At least, I hoped it would have or my ego might not have stood her next test. "You missed it, every time, didn't you? I knew you were there, Walker. I was dancing for you."

The ability to breathe left me. My brain stopped churning. But other parts of my anatomy got with the picture pretty damn fast as I crossed the kitchen to stand right in front of her, looking down at the red headed bombshell who had walked into my life and rearranged it on a whim.

"That was for me, huh?" I murmured.

"Yep." She licked her lips and looked up at me. "So what are you gonna do about that, Walker Roan?"

My hands closed on her hips, and I lifted her tiny frame up onto my kitchen bench to sit in front of me. The borrowed shirt she wore rode up to expose her thighs and before she could think about it too hard, I stepped between her legs, holding her open. My hands skated along the insides of her thighs, pushing her wider as I turned her words over in my head.

"You danced for me. This morning?" I inhaled her sweet scent and knew my clothes would never lose that. Not that I gave a fuck. She nodded slowly. I lifted one hand to coil in her hair, winding the long cherry wood red strands around my fist until I reached her shoulder and tugged a little harder than usual. A soft gasp left her lips. "You danced for me in your fucking underwear, Faith, knowing I watched you. What kind of an invitation was that?"

Her lips parted on a shattered breath. "The sort I wished you took me up on days ago, Walker," she whispered, trailing her fingertips along my wrist where I held her hair hostage, though she didn't try to uncurl my fingers or push me away.

My hand on her thigh pushed higher, until I rubbed my thumb against the scalloped edges of her gold lace panties. "I wish these were white so I could see if you had a wet spot. When we go down to town I'm gonna buy you some," I promised her.

Her breath, already shallow, hitched as her thighs trembled for me.

"You'll come into town with me?"

"Negotiate with me later, Faith," I murmured. "Right now, if I can't see that little wet spot, you sure as fuck better make me feel it, or I'm gonna make you sit here on this cold, hard as fuck bench while I play with you until I do."

Her moan as I stroked along her lacy panties hardened me painfully, and this time, I wasn't disappointed. The slick of her arousal coated my fingers as I toyed with her through the thin lace, the scent of her need heady as she filled my kitchen with the scent of sex, and we hadn't started yet.

"Please, Walker," she whispered, straining against my hand, rubbing herself on my fingers.

I smiled slightly. "You can do better than that," I mocked. "I watched you dance, remember? So dance for me."

Another moan left her as I tugged the borrowed shirt over her head and tossed it on the floor. Mine followed, but her body already undulated for me in a full body roll that did all the right things in all the right places. Faith might dress like a good girl and work her ass off, but she danced like a stripper on demand.

Actually...

I leaned close to her ear, flicking my tongue out to lick the shell as I played with her lace covered pussy and whispered terrible things to the girl I was about to fuck hard.

"Does my little dancer moonlight at some of the bars in White Cap? Do you do it because you're bored, Precious, or for money?"

Her pupils dilated—out of fear, arousal at being called on her bullshit, or a bit of both, I wasn't sure. But it only took a second and she nodded.

"Yes," she whispered, lowering her head in shame.

I caught her chin, forcing her gaze up to meet

mine. "I don't give a fuck if you've danced before. Do what you want to do, and enjoy it. Love it. But right now, from now on, maybe, you dance for me, Faith. Understand?"

Eyes wide, she nodded again, sweating on my counter as she began to move, but it wasn't the same as before. This time she actually began to *move* and I saw why she might choose to spend sleepless nights at some strip joint when she could be home on her own.

Because the girl I was fast falling fall could fucking well *dance*.

I groaned aloud as she undulated, scooting across the benchtop toward me when I nodded my permission to grind her pussy against my denim covered crotch. Her shoulders dropped back, her eyes half closed as she lost herself to music only she could hear.

And when she tipped her head back, arching with her hands knotted in my shirt, I leaned down and claimed a taste of her mouth for the first time.

And damn, was I fucked.

Because one kiss and I was drunk on this woman.

Her lips parted with an explosion of sweetness, all mountain fresh and rainwater from staying with me for the last week and plus some as she leaned into the kiss, letting me devour her with no resistance whatsoever. Her arms linked around my neck, nails lightly scraping over the ink there that had long began to fade.

And all the time, her body rubbed up against mine while she continued to dance for me.

I dropped a hand between us, sliding my fingers over her lace overed breast, thumbing her taut nipple until she moaned, her head tipping back. Then I headed south for her needy little pussy that I wanted to fill.

But slowly, or I risked hurting her. It had been a long time since I was with a woman, and I knew I was above average size for most of them. Faith...she was so damn tiny. I didn't want to hurt her.

My thumbs hooked into the strings at the side of her panties, and I pulled them down her thighs, dropping to my knees between her legs.

"No, I need you," she keened, scraping her nails across my scalp where I'd shorn my hair short.

"I'm not going anywhere, Precious," I promised her, leaning in to flick my tongue across her glistening little hole. "Spread wide for me, so I can make you nice and ready, alright?"

She whimpered as I pressed my tongue to her

entrance and fucked her quickly, raising her hips to meet my thrusts. I licked up her juices the moment she made more, loving her walls fluttering around my tongue. Her plump pussy lips were sensitive, too. I took my time, memorizing what made her moan, working my way up to her clit.

The moment I sucked the little nub into my mouth, I pushed one thick finger inside her, and she fucking detonated on me, slow and endless. Her hips rocked as she fucked herself on my hand, everything inside her tightening like she couldn't stop. I added another finger, pumping hard until she bowed backward, lifting her hips off the counter. I pushed a hand to her hips, pressing her back down and worked her until she screamed my name.

Then I hit repeat, sucking on her clit until she writhed for me, and added my finger to her weeping pussy again. Her hands fluttered at my shoulders, but I refused to stop until her body softened under the onslaught of pleasure, the highness in her pussy easing a little as she came on my tongue and hand again and again.

Then I lifted her hips as I pushed up from my knees and stepped between them, lining myself up with her tender flesh. "You tell me if I'm hurting you, Precious," I whispered.

Her lips found mine as she licked her juices from my mouth, and I swore I nearly came on the spot. "Break me, Walker."

I kissed her hard, slamming my mouth over hers and thrust my tongue roughly between her lips even as I slid my cock slowly into her tight, welcoming pussy. Although I'd spent time preparing her, her pussy was a snug fit. She whined, shifting as I held her close, impaling her on my length. Her body flexed and tightened as she came again without help this time and I plunged all the way inside her still fluttering pussy. Her soaked walls aided my intrusion as she gasped and choked against my shoulder.

"Breathe, Faith," I instructed, cupping my hand behind her head. She still wore the damn bra. I fumbled the clip, wishing I could rip it off her but she barely had any clothes left as it was. I managed to unclip the lacy thing and pulled it free of her body, pressing her bare skin to mine. "Better," I murmured, stroking her back. "Yeah?"

"So much better." She sighed her pleasure in the circle of my arms, rocking her hips as I moved slowly within her.

I leaned back, checking her face for winces, but she never showed one fragment of pain.

"You take all of me so fucking well, Faith." My voice strained as I looked between us.

Her pussy swallowed all of me, over and over as I pushed inside her tight body, gripping her hips and plunging deeper every time. Her juices squirted around us, coating her thighs and my jeans, dripping over my balls, but I didn't care.

Luminous, color change eyes lifted to meet mine. "I'll clean you up with my tongue later," she whispered, leaning up to lick my bottom lip with the tip of her tongue.

I snarled and smashed our mouths together, gripping her hips tight as I swore she'd designed and fucked her hard. Three thrusts was all it took and she was trembling in my hands as she came again, clenching down on my cock and soaking up both.

"Fuck, Presh—" I groaned, my balls drawing up tight. "You feel too good—"

Too late I remembered I wasn't wearing protection. My seed branded her walls, deep inside her as my orgasm ripped through me, so good it was almost painful. My roar echoed off the mountainside and the finally abating rain as I held Faith in my arms, enjoying the way she trembled for me way too fucking much.

And tried to plan how I could keep her with me for a few more days before I had to take her back to civilization and all the things I never wanted to deal with ever again.

Right now, I had a beautiful woman in my arms who orgasmed on demand, and we had only just started. Surely a few extra days wouldn't hurt anyone.

CHAPTER SEVEN

FAITH

I knew Walker lied about the mountain not being passable for the next three days as he kept me in his house and fucked me every waking hour. I knew, and I didn't object to a single minute of it. We had just found each other, and my mini-mountain God wasn't the sort of man I was inclined to argue with.

Not that I was scared of him. Sure, Walker Roan could be terrifyingly intimidating if he so chose, but he rarely showed that side to me—so far. What I wanted was to fall asleep in his arms, wake up before him and show my mountain man just what having a woman in his life might add to his solitary existence.

This morning's session involved cockwarming. Which was a personal kink at the top of my list. I had no idea if he'd be into it, but I woke him with his cock in my mouth, simply keeping him warm as he stretched and stroked my hair and shoulders.

"Fuck, that feels good, Precious," he murmured, winding my hair around his fist and guiding my head gently.

I shook my head, and leaned my cheek against his stomach, keeping still.

He stopped, considered, and let me do my thing, leaning back. Slowly, his cock hardened in my mouth. I licked and suckled gently to prevent from drooling on occasion, and he sighed, resting back, his legs supporting me as I held him in my mouth.

"Good girl." Walker stroked my cheek gently with his knuckles.

I moaned. Hell, I almost came when he uttered those two golden worlds. His hand dropped to my breast where he played idly with my nipple, and I started to realize the position I'd put myself in as my arousal level peaked. I twisted but he refused to stop and so I sucked him gently, needing to ease the growing ache between my legs as he toyed with my nipples, milking me one at a time. The long moan he drew from my lips when he tapped my head, reminding me of my silent vow to be still, nearly floored me.

I protested, but he laughed and when he pushed deep into my throat, one hand pressed firm to the back of my head, I was trapped.

"Thssaasssaaabbbdddddeaa," I mumbled around my mouthful of cock, sticking my tongue out to lave his balls.

"Fuck, that's good, Precious." Walker contented himself with playing with my hair and stroking my back after that. I resigned myself to the fate I'd set up for until he slid his hands down my body and set me upright on his hips to straddle him, letting me stretch my legs. "I want to see you fuck me. Slowly," he warned, his eyes hard in warning not to defy him.

Intimidating as all hell.

I knew he worried about hurting me, and I got it —his cock was as thick as my wrist. But Walker Roan had a tendency to make me come a dozen times before we screwed or, like this morning, to tease the absolute fuck out of us both until I was a sopping, whining, writhing mess.

Either way, I was more than ready by the time he pushed into me. Or in this case, I slid over him, taking him all the way inside me before I stopped, breathless, my thighs resting on top of his.

"Oh, wow," I whispered, finding his gaze with my slightly wild one. "That's— wow, Walker."

"Are you okay, Faith?" he checked in, cupping my cheeks and leaned forward to kiss me tenderly. "Tell me you're okay?"

"I'm okay," I reassured him. "Fine. Just getting used to youuuuu–"

My whisper became a wail as he clamped both hands onto my hips and railed me from below, ripping control from my hands and slammed into me until I grabbed at his shoulders in a bid to cling to *something*.

Everything disappeared as my entire body shook with the force of his thrusts. I left half-moon shaped scrapes on his chest and shoulders as I tried to grasp a hand hold to him and failed. Then my orgasm rammed into me—or maybe he did—and I stopped thinking about scratching him at all. My body tightened as I arched against him. Juices dripped down my thighs where we joined.

The first time I squirted on him, I thought he had come already. But when I did it time and again with him in the same session, I realized his body somehow hit something inside me that just brought out the maximum amount of pleasure. Walker made sure I stayed hydrated afterwards, too.

I leaned down and kissed him, finding his mouth and parting my lips for his tongue. His kisses were rough and deep, just like the way he fucked. Everything about Walker was in proportion, as advertised for any good lumber snack. And oh, hell, what a lumber snack. I cried into his shoulder when what he did became too much in an overwhelm of mountain man proportions, but I refused to beg him to stop.

If our time together was limited—and I couldn't think about that right now—then I wanted to preserve every memory we could make in the next hours. Our bodies slammed together over and over. I coated us both with my cum before he growled in my ear words that my lust addled brain struggled to make out.

Then his mouth was back on mine and he flipped us both, slamming hilt deep as he came inside me. His hips jerked once, my name on his lips as he held me close. My breath formed his name on a plea, an echo that refused to die.

I sank into the circle of his arms and let Walker Roan block out reality for me for one more day.

"We'll head down the mountain today."

I closed my eyes and pretended my tame lumber snack hadn't just stripped away my happiness privileges. I mean, I knew we had to go back, but I'd enjoyed the break from the life I forced myself into because it's what I was supposed to do.

After all, I was *supposed* to work my butt off. I was *supposed* to get a law degree. I was *supposed* to be this kick ass girl with the brain to match and beat all the boys at their own game because of the gifts given to me.

All the pressures I never caved under that I got to release in a week and a bit in the shelter of Walker Roan. And in a scant handful of words he stripped all that comfort away that I craved and threw it off a mountainside like so much junk.

Worst thing? He had no idea because like with every other problem I'd faced in my life, I said absolutely nothing and kept on dancing.

Right at his kitchen bench with a fake as fuck smile plastered on my face that I'd worn for so long that it had become my real one.

"Fantastic. I'll go pack my stuff." I stayed right

where I was and threw Walker a blindingly bright grin as I tucked my dead phone into my back pocket.

Good thing I wore my own clothes today.

Especially since I'd made a habit of wearing one of his shirts and nothing else for the last few days while we fucked around his house and both pretended that this was life and nothing else mattered.

For the last forty-eight hours, nothing else had.

Walker's eyes narrowed on me. "Sassy little thing," he muttered, turning into the pantry.

A tactical looking backpack was gripped in his hand that had a long black cord-like thing hanging out of it. He stopped, reversed, and filled the satchel with water. Then he pivoted on his heel and headed back the way he'd started originally.

My breath stalled. "Wait, you mean on foot?" What remained of my good humor deserted me.

Walker's snort echoed through the pantry, along his crazy circular mountain home and back to me. "Did you think we were going to hire a plane and fly you out in luxury, Precious? Yeah, we're walkin'."

"Ah." I swallowed, forcing my smile back onto my face, though it felt less real this time. "You don't have a pair of boots I can borrow, do you?"

"Maybe with a few pairs of socks." He reappeared holding a stack of power bars and meal supplements that looked like cardboard and probably tasted the same. "I've got an old pair of Trav's. He's not as big as me—"

I stared at him, aghast. "The man is six foot and six inches tall!" Mind, I reckoned that Walker capped out at around just shy of seven feet. What in the hell was I complaining about?

"—And you might be able to fit into this with some...help." He ignored my outburst and kept on packing. A tube of sun cream bounced my way. "Put that on. I've got a hat, but it's not going to stay on that little pinhead of yours."

I glared at him. "I beg your pardon?"

Walker smirked. "Come on, Precious. Don't we have a business of yours to get you back to?"

My stomach swooped. "Yeah. Cause That's the stuff that really matters, right?" I grabbed the sunscreen, lathering it on and cursed the rain for ever stopping.

"Did you fall out of the wrong side of my bed this morning, Faith?"

I didn't need to look at him to know that Walker was frowning at me, his inked face scrunched up like one of those roly-poly dogs.

"Nope." I kept on slathering.

"Whoa. Slow down there." He liberated the cream and placed it gently back on the bench. "You wanna talk to me?"

I laughed at my hands covered in an excess of white goop. "Nope."

"That's something new." He sighed. "Pee. Drink a lot of water. It'll be dark before we reach Red Hart, but we'll get most of the hike done before the sun sets. I'll carry an extra jacket for you."

I glared at his back as he turned away from me. "I'll carry my own things."

"Suit yourself."

His shoulders lifted in a shrug, his irritation a match for my own. *We're more alike than you think, Walker Roan.*

He hadn't been privy to the conversations I shared with his father over the years when there was no one else to listen to the lonely old man talk. Because while Walker seconded himself away from the world, his father was a social butterfly...until he wasn't.

Until life took away his open intentions and locked a suddenly old man away in his own body and mind, and a small town like White Cap started to forget that he ever existed.

The irony was that Walker wanted what his

father achieved by accident. The role reversal wasn't lost on me, or the old man I visited on a weekly basis. By the end of the first month I had a tea collection to rival a foreign court, because that's what his father drank. Every month I added to it, and we shared stories—-or at least, he did while I listened. Collected his memories so that one day, I might share some of those stories with the son who left after they fought, and never came back.

And now, I had one day left and I hadn't done the real job I came to do when I decided to invade the mountain where Walker Roan hid himself away years ago in a bid to make sure that the world forgot he existed.

And I still didn't know why any more than his father did.

Because Walker never told him, either.

A cough brought me out of my thoughts. "We need to leave, Faith."

Walker stood a few feet away from me, two jackets clipped to the backpack strung across his ridiculously broad, muscular shoulders that his black tee did nothing to hide.

Lumber snack, activated.

I nodded. "I'm ready."

He held out three pairs of thick, woolen socks and kicked muddied boots my way. "Almost."

I nodded, planting my butt on the floor without argument. He was ready to go. There was no point fighting. We were done, clearly. Lacing my borrowed footwear up as best I could around my ankles under his watchful eye, I declared myself ready a second time.

Walker said nothing, raking his gaze over me. His eyes lingered on my lips. For a moment I thought he might kiss me, but he seemed to have shut that part of us off the moment he made the choice to push me out of his house.

I swallowed hard. We really were done. The fun part of this unintentional mountain segue was over, and I was being evicted out of his life. I turned on the heel of my borrowed boots to stare out at the view I could finally see that went on and on and on over the pine forests. Cold air lit my lungs with a need to stare for hours and absorb everything.

From here, if I stepped close enough to the edge, it felt like I was flying.

"Faith," Walker murmured, close enough his breath brushed the back of my nape exposed where I'd piled my hair on my head in a horrendously messy bun because out here, being neat and perfect didn't matter.

I nodded, soaking in one more breath of the stunning vista like I could imprint some of its untouched, brutal crispness into my skin. Then I turned my back on everything that was perfect in his world, and followed the man I'd already fallen for off his mountain knowing I'd never see any of it ever again.

CHAPTER EIGHT

WALKER

I stared down the face of the mountain that looked both the same since I last used this track and had changed in all the ways that was usual for this time of year. The rain had eroded a lot of the gathered pine needle mulch, washed away a few saplings trying to garner a foothold with scant roots at this altitude.

The landslip that we had experienced when Faith first arrived at my place wasn't the only one that we spotted, the path giving way to unstable ground under the last week of rain and deluge of water cascading down the mountainside in impromptu waterfalls and random trickles. The sight would have been stunning but deadly had we left earlier, and I was glad we waited to head down to Red Hart.

Not that we had a choice. The path would have been impassable until now. Even so, we gave the fallen rocks a large berth. But none of that was what bothered me.

What hurt was Faith's silence that followed me from my house all the way to the halfway point I aimed for nearly six hours after we left—an hour later than I intended thanks to the argument about the boots. I figured she'd get tired fast and that we'd cover more ground in the morning than the afternoon. No matter how many times I helped her, praised her, or fed her, Faith kept herself to herself.

Which was nothing like the woman I thought I knew. Who I was fast falling for in the weeks she'd lived in my home. A short time where we'd been on top of each other—sometimes literally—and I'd learned a hell of a lot about her.

Rule number one: Faith had zero filter. What she thought came straight out of her mouth.

Which meant her silence was fucking unnerving.

Even I could see she was bursting to say something. But whatever Faith Somerset wanted to tell me, she kept tightly under wraps for the first time since I'd met her.

If she'd been this quiet on that first day, things might have gone very differently in my house.

Now that I knew what she tasted like when she kissed me, what she felt like when I held her or how she cried after we fucked when she thought I'd fallen asleep, I understood how rare a gift her silence was.

And what a curse.

Because those were the times that I held onto her and refused to let her go, her lithe tight body pressed to mine, silent tears collecting on my chest in tiny pools.

If she wanted to talk to me and tell me her secrets, whisper them to me as the rain fell, she would have. But she kept those too, her fears turning inward and cried herself to sleep then, too. Just as she walked in silence now.

The problem was that her secrets weren't just eating at her.

They ate at me, too.

Finally, as I helped her haul her perfect little ass —that I knew the shape of intimately, because the feel of her was still molded into my palms from our playtime during the night before—over a shattered section of granite from a long prior rock slide, my patience died a short and sharp death.

"Spit it out, Precious," I muttered, wrapping my hand around her hip and gave her a quick slap.

Faith let out the sweetest as fuck growl that boiled my blood. Instead of giving her the desired boost forward over the split boulder where I was supposed to be helping her, I tugged her back against me.

Her back pressed to my chest, and her ass ground against my groin, leaving me aching and hard, a state I'd been trying my damn best to avoid since we started walking hours ago.

She hadn't whined or bitched at me once. Not when she slipped and grazed her hands when I hadn't been watching her close enough, or when her socks got soaked crossing a stream that hadn't been there last time I used the track. Her feet had to be covered in blisters from the boots that were far too big for her feet, but still she kept her silence, and more than that, my girl kept up with me.

I hadn't been as impressed with another human since I saw my father take on the local bureaucrats as a twenty something. Or the month after when I walked out—or he kicked me out, depending on who you spoke to back then—and headed up the mountain after I negotiated with Red Hart for the land. Trav and Jude put in a summer's worth of work with me for the hell of it, and to get the hell out of Trav's dad's hair for two months solid.

That was a short, tight list, and Faith just topped it.

"Spit what out?" she snarked at me, pushing her weight back into me before she launched forward.

"Easy, Presh." I was ready for her, wrapping my arm around her waist and holding on tight.

Faith thrashed for a long moment, but her energy was well down, and she stopped fighting me, though her nails dug into my exposed forearm where I'd rolled my sleeves back.

"I thought you were taking me back, not holding me hostage, Mister Roan."

I winced at the title. "Did you use that name with my father?"

She stalled against me, her chest heaving. "No, actually. I called him by his first name."

My eyebrows shot into my hairline. "You called him Chaz?"

Faith shrugged. "He asked me to. So why not?" she challenged me. "Was that an attorney-client privilege I shouldn't have been using, or did you give up your rights when you walked away years before?"

Damn, she was pissed at me. I still didn't let her go. She smelled too good. Felt good, too, pressed right up against me. I inhaled deeply, running my nose along the length of her throat and buried my face in her neck.

Her body stiffened, but the strangled moan that slipped from her lips was unmissable. I loosened my hold around her stomach and she didn't pull away.

"You don't get to ask questions like that, Miss Somerset," I murmured, licking the shell of her ear while she made more of those sweet little noises for me.

The woman who could be so hard and tough curved her body against mine. Faith went all soft and sweet, so different from the snarky woman she'd been a moment before. I'd learned her body, who she was over the last days, and taken my time understanding what she needed. What scared her. What made her cling to me and beg for more even if she was too fuck-drunk to remember telling me.

"Walker—" she whispered, her voice a bare thread, but I didn't let her finish.

"I walked away from my father because I could never be who he was. Who everyone expected me to be. Because I couldn't be him, Precious. I was always the silent version, the ultimate disappointment in his eyes." I shrugged as she spun in my arms, the fine lines around her eyes tightening. "Surprised I don't have a better reason for hiding from the world?" *For running away?*

Her mouth opened and shut twice, and stayed that way.

Faith, speechless? That's new.

I leaned in and stole a kiss before I could think the better of it. Her hand cupped my cheek, then she shoved me back hard, gasping.

"Hell, no. Not after you pull me out of your house like you did this morning. Fuck you," she muttered, yanking out of my arms and pivoting to continue climbing the rock pile on her own.

I smirked at her ass wiggling in my face. "Is that what you're upset about, Precious? You thought you wouldn't get an invitation back?"

Her derisive laughter might have iced my veins if I hadn't recognized the hurt beneath that tone. "As if I want to risk coming back up your mountain and getting swept away. Again."

I reached out and placed a hand on her lower back where she slipped, steadying her. "I'll replace your car with something that can," I promised her. It wasn't like my bank account wasn't overflowing. I took in money from what I earned trading hand crafted goods for Kyle and a few others, and hard labor for Red Hart and a few neighbors. Where the fuck would I spend any of it? "Or something that can't. Whatever you need. That's on me for not coming down when I knew you were looking for me years ago."

She batted my hand away. "Fuck you, Roan."

"Already did that, Presh."

She flipped me the bird and landed on the other side of the rock pile with an *oof*. Then there was nothing but silence.

I frowned. "You okay, Faith?" I waited a beat. "Faith?" I hauled myself over the boulder and landed on the other side on both feet, missing her outspread hand that rested beside her by scant inches. "Shit. Sorry, girl."

But her attention wasn't on me or where my boots landed. Her gaze was fixed on what lay to the west beyond where the track turned as she slowly pushed herself up to standing without turning to acknowledge me at all.

Here, the trees opened out, the mountain turning away to present the first look out over Red Hart and the land beyond that scooped down into the wide valley where the ranch house sat.

The river where Eve and Rhys found sapphires

ran well below us, far enough I couldn't hear its rushing, swollen waters after rain. That would be an ass to cross, but we'd manage. Then the forest and the grassy plains on Beaumont land that the twins now owned between them, prime grazing land that bordered on Black Hill land. On the other side of the rise to my west lay trader Kyle's new family.

I'd come up here to hide away from the world and somehow managed to learn all the politics and family entanglements of the locals thanks to then-two young cowboys who took it upon themselves to help a lonely, heartbroken man because they decided he shouldn't be left alone after all.

Faith gazed out over the ranch, the work of generations of Trav and Eve's family. Her long red hair streamed down her back where it had come loose from her top notch hours ago. She swept one hand through the wayward strands and reached back for me absently.

"It's so beautiful," she whispered.

It's beautiful.

She'd said that the first night she stayed at my place, watching the rain crash in sheets against the cliff face, pattering against her bare feet. I'd thought the same thing then, watching the fire and pretending not to watch her, only my thoughts hadn't been directed to the rain.

"So are you." I swallowed hard, my voice as thin and thready as hers had been before. Maybe Jude and Trav hadn't been so wrong all those years ago after all. It just took me all this long to figure it out. "Yeah, it is," I finally whispered loud enough for her to hear as I slid my fingers around hers and clasped them firmly.

She let out a little gasp, but didn't look away from the view. Not when I stepped up behind her or dropped the backpack on the ground. Not when I slid my other hand around her waist and tucked her back against me.

Or when I drew our entwined fingers to her chin, tipped her head back to find her eyes already closed, and sealed my mouth over hers.

Fuck, I'm falling for a girl I can't keep.

The belated thought strayed across my mind as I gathered her into my arms and dipped a knee to lay her out on the jackets I'd brought with us. I fumbled to spread the material out beneath her before her head hit the stone, her head decorating the speckled granite like a fiery halo.

Faith's sighs lit a deep need inside me. I kissed her long, but not rough, needing this last memory with her. She was right; I'd tried to keep it clean this morning and say goodbye without doing it right when we left.

I'd been a coward then.

Now, I had a chance to make that up to her. My mouth melded to hers as she lifted her hips, letting me peel her white jeans to her knees and positioned myself between her soft thighs. It was a tight fit, but I shoved my own pants aside and pushed a finger inside her to find her sopping for me already.

I opened my mouth to speak, but she raised her head, kissing the needless words away. Her moan reverberated against my lips as I teased her with a few shallow thrusts, then replaced my finger with my cock, pushing inside her long and deep. Her mouth broke from mine on the sort of keening cry that echoed from the mountain's high walls. I breathed hard, lost in her eyes that reflected the sunlight and dappled shade all at once as her hands flexed around my neck, her nails digging into my skin.

My cock swelled painfully as I rubbed my knuckles against the hard stone beneath her, using the pain as I distraction so I'd last inside her luscious fucking heat. Her whimpers drove me on, but I kept my pace steady, needing to memorize the feel of her, every flutter as she rolled her hips with me.

Faith's first climax drifted sweetly over us, coating me in her cream as I bit my tongue against the glorious sensation of being drenched raw inside her as she came. I found her eyes, registering the tears already there.

"Am I hurting you?" I murmured, brushing the drops away with my thumb.

She shook her head. "I don't want this to stop. Not ever."

My heart sang as I gripped her hip and pushed deeper then withdrew slowly, setting the sort of rhythm that wouldn't let me come until I was ready.

But Faith...she unfurled around me, her edge of bliss already leaving her clenching on my cock as I drowned her cries with my kisses. For once, we weren't rough.

The silent mountain alone bore witness to the slow brand of love that I etched soul deep in the girl I'd fallen for in the hope that one day, she might remember the way I made her feel, and love me back.

CHAPTER NINE

FAITH

Darkness descended over the foothills of the mountain in a slow shadow that chased us through Red Hart lands for the last hours of our hike back toward semi-civilization. My legs burned like fuck. I could barely see ten feet in front of us, but at least I didn't have to do this last bit alone.

Because after Walker spent the better part of the afternoon—when I knew we didn't really have time to waste—making love to me spread out on a pair of his jackets, he wrapped his hand around mine and refused to let go. Hell, he even held on tight all the time that he fed me, making sure I ate plenty and drank enough water.

We still didn't talk much on the walk back, but something changed after that. Rather than fight against each other with a hyper awareness of the other's presence, he was just...there.

The whole time.

When my legs ached and placing one foot before the other became too much, he squeezed my hand, shortened his pace and made sure I followed him without dragging me along the path. He didn't pressure me, and he didn't go too easy on me, either.

I held onto that lifeline he offered, and I didn't let go.

So that was how we arrived at Red Hart's big house nearly two weeks after I left, passing a line of farm hands who looked like they were done for the day, more than one clutching an after dinner beer that I knew Eve served at her usually over-laden table.

"I think we missed the best part of the night," I murmured to Walker behind a yawn.

"I'm sure there will be leftovers." He squeezed my hand.

His rough calluses and warmth were a staunch reminder of the strength that got us down what should have been a damn hard walk. My mountain man made it seem easy even when my body made me want to plant my butt and never move ever again.

"Always are." Gage, one of the live-in ranch hands, and his fiancé, Brit, paused beside us, his arm slung around her body as she leaned into him. "Heard you were coming down the mountain." He held out a hand.

Walker hesitated, his hand flexing tight on mine for a moment. It hit me in one just how easy going we had been together and what being in public actually cost him.

I pressed my body against his back as he shook Gage's hand briefly before pulling back and winding me tightly into his side.

"I have to get someone food and a bed," he muttered gruffly.

Gage inclined his head. "Understood," he murmured, and I remembered he'd been a soldier at some point, too.

Maybe Red Hart and the lands surrounding the ranch house had a draw for a certain personality type.

"Are you going to be okay with this many people around?" I asked Walker, pulling back, but he wouldn't let me.

"We'll find out." His arm tightened on me, almost to the point of uncomfortable.

I didn't say anything or shift away, stealing a little more of his warmth for the last minutes I had him to myself. My hands slid inside his jacket, pressing to the hard ridges of his stomach as I closed my eyes and hummed something noncommittal against his chest.

Some of the tension left his tense frame. He pressed a kiss to the top of my head. "You gonna show me that fancy office of yours in White Cap tomorrow?"

I broke out of my cuddle zone and jerked my head up to stare at his face. "You'll come into town with me? Borrow a truck?"

He shrugged. "I might have left a truck here with Jude one year."

My mouth fell open.

Walker shut it gently with two fingers. "Bugs'll get in this time of night, Precious."

I leaned my head against his shoulder and ignored the line of farm hands who stared openly at us. "You are full of surprises, Walker Roan."

His chest rumbled as we approached the big house. "I ain't the only one."

Jude's silhouette leaning against the wide veranda was easy to spot. "Heard you were coming down. One of the boys ran back to tell me." His voice held no more of a smile than the slice of his face that I could see in the reflected light from the house as he looked at me. "We were waiting for the rain to stop, Faith. Knew you'd be safe with him, because otherwise he would have come down, even if it meant coming in during the rain. I tried to call, but—"

"My phone went flat pretty fast. I know. That's on me. I should have listened." I leaned into Walker's side and hugged him tight. He held on and didn't make me face Jude alone, thankfully, because now it was my turn to be the cowardly lion. "I'm sorry, Jude."

He didn't rip me a new one, and I was grateful. "Looks like you were in good hands."

I nodded while Walker stroked my hair. "I was." *I am.* If he was coming into town with me tomorrow, I'd bought one more day with the mountain man who I didn't want to leave any time soon.

A day in town. Hell, he freaked out when a farm hand he knew at least in passing shook his hand. How was he going to go in a ton with a population of approximately five thousand people? I mean, they weren't all going to flock to him at once, but my office was on the main street. I'd been gone for over a week with no notice. People would be dropping by.

I bit my lip and cast those thoughts out of my mind. I'd deal with tomorrow...well, tomorrow.

"Need a feed?" Jude still hadn't moved, and I got the impression we were yet to pass some sort of unspoken test before the foreman would let us into the domain he protected for the twins.

"Glad to see you made it out safe." Travis walked out of the big house and down the steps of the veranda, wiping his hands on a tea towel. "Eve's heating up some food for you. There's plenty left. How much can you eat, Faith?" His gaze lingered on where Walker's arm wrapped around me.

"A bit," I mumbled through another yawn.

"Good," Travis said approvingly. "Eve's got rooms made up for you."

Walker's hand stopped stroking my hair. "We'll stay together."

Jude made an all-male noise in his throat, turned on his heel, and disappeared into the house. Walker seemed to take that as an invitation, kicking off his boots at the step and held out a hand for me to do the same. A frisson of heat that had nothing to do with sex and everything to do with my heart rippled through me. I leaned on his arm for balance as I untied my borrowed footwear and tried to breathe evenly.

"That's okay with you, Faith?" Travis asked softly, unmoving from his spot, still wiping his hands with the tea towel. "Staying with the big guy?"

I looked up at the Walker, who hadn't taken his eyes off me, and I nodded.

"Yeah," I managed, noting the way Walker's gaze darkened possessively at my answer. My stomach flipped in a way that had nothing at all to do with my exhaustion, food, or the lack of it.

"I'll stay with him."

Over an hour later we were filled with more food than I ever expected to be fed, especially when we had rocked up unannounced to someone's house at ten o'clock in the evening after the literal hoards had already been through the kitchen for the night. Eve fed us a veritable feast, Travis and Jude joining in for seconds. Walker devoured his usual house-sized version of a meal, and I managed more than I expected despite my eyelids drooping at the table. Then, Eve brought out dessert. I decided afterwards that as good as the vanilla slice tasted, I never wanted to see it ever again.

Afterward they let us say goodnight, Travis and Jude talking quietly at the long table after we all cleaned up while Eve settled in the leather sofa by the fire to message her long distance boyfriend with a promise that she'd laid out a set of both night clothes and an outfit I could have for tomorrow.

Walker hauled me up the stairs as my legs finally decided they had enough, sliding his arms around my waist and lifting me onto his hips in a bear hug. I didn't object, wrapping my arms around his neck and burrowing into him, recalling all too well the way his body pressed mine into the mountain as he claimed me beneath its eye, it seemed, this afternoon.

Or maybe I was being all fanciful, but that was what it seemed like he had done. I was half asleep by the time he led us into the spare bedroom at the end of the hall upstairs in the big house, surrounded by his familiar scent and his strength. My new safe place.

Walker kicked the door shut behind us and

carried me past the bed, keeping my legs wrapped around his waist and headed straight into the ensuite, already peeling my top over my head. I moaned as his mouth connected with mine in a deep, rough kiss that tasted of his last coffee and the remnants of vanilla slice with a dusting of sugar.

My tongue slid across his lips as he placed me carefully against the bench, unbuttoning my jeans and slid them over my hips. I doubted they were white any more, or that they were recoverable. I didn't care either way as he pushed them over my legs, along with my panties, and discarded our clothes on the floor. My bra went next. Then one hand held me to him as he reached into the shower and flicked the hot water on and whispered the sexiest words I'd ever heard in my ear.

"I'm gonna hold you up while I wash your hair, Precious."

I groaned aloud and let him guide me under the water which was *almost* scalding hot as promised. Walker carried out his oath to perfection, his thick, strong fingers massaging my scalp as I moaned softly, leaning into him. My legs turned to jelly within seconds. I clung to him, turning around as he needed, letting him work out the knots in my hair and tilted my head back to allow him to wash out the conditioner.

Then he washed me too, cleaning the mess he'd made on me before, soaping me gently. I pried my eyes open, stealing a little soap to glide my hands over him, too. He tried to knock my hands away, but I shook my head.

"I want to touch you," I whispered. "Just a bit?" I yawned again.

"Mmm," he muttered, voicing his opinion in a mountain-worthy rumble that left me giggling.

In the end he let me clean his back and chest and part of his arms, but that was as far as I managed before he quickly finished himself and washed us down, then wrapped me in a fluffy towel, drying my hair.

"You're perfect," I murmured, leaning into his embrace.

"You'll forget about me once you're back at work, Precious." He kissed the corner of my mouth.

I turned into the kiss, melding our lips together, and opened my eyes, finding him, though my vision blurred at the edges from pure exhaustion. "If I don't?" I mumbled.

He didn't pull away. "Then you know where I live."

My breath came short as he lifted me in his arms, discarded the towel, and placed me in the bed, both of us naked. Walker pulled me into his body, kissing me deeply, his arms wrapped around me, until I fell asleep.

Safe and warm and together.

CHAPTER TEN

WALKER

I hated crowds. It was one of the reasons I left White Cap in the first fucking place. People crawled everywhere. If I had thought Red Hart was busy this morning before Faith and I escaped the big house with all of its twenty-two ranch hands and live in cowboys and assorted families, it had nothing on the chaos of the town I left behind over a decade ago. White Cap had more than doubled in size in the time that I had been gone.

Apparently, Faith's unannounced absence was a big damn deal. The locals needed to know she was safe. Returned unharmed. People touched her. Hugged her. Bought her coffee. The newspaper turned up and took her picture, for fuck's safe. The police, I understood. Even the radio station decided to get in on the act.

Some of the shops near her business decided to poke their noses in. Clients brought her flowers. She didn't die. Okay, so her car made headlines. She wasn't in it. But you know who never turned up? Family. Friends. Those people seemed to be missing from her life.

Because Faith Somerset, in the pursuit of her career, had foregone all the things that others lived for, while she existed solely for work.

I wandered around her private office space, the door shut between me and her, while her not friends and family visited for the first three fucking hours we were in White Cap because I couldn't stand the noise. Or the company. I understood what she was doing, but fuck me if it didn't annoy the shit out of me that she had to hide me away from the world because I couldn't be there beside her when she was overrun with people who, as far as I could tell, she didn't want around her in the first place.

Well, not most of them.

Finally, Faith managed to free herself of the crowd and stumbled into her own office holding yet another flower and a stack of takeaway coffees, one atop each other like a tower.

"Here. I don't know what flavor that is, but it's yours."

I eyed the fancy pink cup she held out to me. "Why do I suspect this has a whole lotta sugar in it, Faith?"

"Probably does," she admitted. "But it's yours, now. Drink it or dump it. I do not give a single fuck."

I leaned in and kissed her. Her eyes opened wide before she sank into me, her lips parting on a sigh. I took that invitation, deepened the kiss and wished I had fucked her the night before. But she'd been shattered, and holding her that night had been the right way to treat her. Still, I had fantasies that I wanted to play out with this woman, and the time we had together on my mountain hadn't been anywhere near enough.

Waking up with her wrapped around me this morning...that had been its own moment to treasure. Her glorious red hair spread across us both, her legs tangled around mine, my hand curved over the swell over her ass.

Everything I hadn't realized I missed from my life, because I hated being around people.

Or maybe I just wanted one.

Her.

"I wish we could start today again." She echoed my thoughts to perfection.

"Could do," I murmured against her lips, drawing back to look into her color change eyes. Here, away from the mountain, the greens were dulled. "You gonna take me out to see the land later on?"

Her eyes flared wide, and a flush rose up her cheeks. "Walker? Something you need to tell me?"

I swallowed hard and nodded. "You wanna tell me why my father's favorite tea is lined along your office back wall?" It wasn't just his favorite tea. My father had five favorite tea brands. More than that, actually. He had an obsession with tea. And I spotted every single one of them on her back wall in a neat line, like she'd ranked them. And right at the end were the ones that contained...

I drew my finger in a line across the fancy tins and stopped at the end without saying a word.

She filled in the blanks for me. "Bergamot." Faith wrinkled her nose. "Chaz hated the ones with berg-amot hidden in them."

"He did. How often was he in here?"

"Monthly. Usually when he came into town. Not that home was far away but you know, ten minutes is far in White Cap. When he stopped being able to come in and he was confined at home, I took the tea to him."

I held onto her tight. "What did you talk about?"

My father talked to everyone, including me. I just... I was never able to talk back. I tried, but I couldn't. It was like a barrier formed between us, impossible to cross. Knowing he had someone he connected with eased some of the guilt weighing on my heart.

"Town. Gossip. Police. Politics. International, local. Your father was interested in—"

"Everything," I finished for her. "I never could keep up."

Her head tipped to one side. "I don't think that's true, Walker. You keep up with me just fine. I think you were scared you might disappoint a man you looked up to, someone you emulated. Your dad was your hero. But you know what?"

Her words rang true. Too true. I swallowed hard. "What?"

She smiled. "You were his hero, too. He was so proud of his boy for going off to the Army. That was something few others here did. You were the one who left. You didn't need anyone else. He used to say that everyone else in White Cap was stuck here.

Right here in this town where they were born with nowhere to go and only the wind of the next house to listen to them chatter. You, Walker? You got up. You ignored everyone else, and you did your own thing. He was so proud of you for leaving. Then you came back, and you made your way up the mountain on your own. He was proud of that, too. I think because he couldn't bring himself to leave, either."

My heart clenched down hard in my chest. I pressed my lips to the top of her head and rested my cheek there as she wrapped her arms around my waist and held on.

"Ovvvuuu," she mumbled into my chest.

I frowned. "Huh?"

"I love you," Walker Roan," she whispered.

"Fuck," I muttered.

"Bless you," she said, pointedly.

"Sorry, Precious.. Just...you can't blindside a man like that." I turned her face up to mine and kissed her hard. "You gave me everything I needed from my dad, and then told me you loved me when I thought I was gonna have to walk away from you today and leave you right here and never see you again. Am I gonna have to do that?"

She shook her head. "Not unless that's what you want."

I watched her eyes, the ones that were dulled a moment before but flared bright with a rainbow of greens and browns now, all the colors of my mountain.

"Fuck, no. I love you too, Faith. Let's see that land and work out what in the hell to do with it."

She sent me the first shy smile I'd ever seen in her. "I have some ideas."

I raised my eyebrows. "I bet you do. Does that come under conflict of interest?"

"Only if I handle it."

I laughed out loud. "You do have a plan for everything, don't you?" I took a slug of the pink coffee and nearly spat it all over her flooring. "Christ, that tastes like cotton candy." I thought I'd forgotten the flavor, but it came rushing back in one and it was worse than ever mixed with burnt, over-priced coffee beans.

Her eyes flashed with mischief as I grabbed for her and crushed our mouths together, kissing her until she was breathless and sharing the love of the sickly sweet coffee.

"Gotcha, mountain man," she whispered.

EPILOGUE

FAITH

Walker's view hadn't changed much since the first day I set foot on his mountain. I had though, and so did the little bundle of life in my belly who grew by the day. I pressed one hand to the top of my belly as I stared out at the light rain that sprinkled the mountain in coolness at the end of autumn, winter's early kiss settling in.

The rock face before me reverberated with Walker's renovations that he promised would be finished before our baby arrived. Not that we would have him—or her—here. He'd kept his promise and set foot on his dad's land for the first time in years, claiming it back for both of us. I had handed the management over to a co-worker I trusted, and we had built the first foundations of our family home there together.

But Walker's home here above Red Hart would always be his, and it would always be somewhere special for us all. Which was why he was currently building a folding wall that would shutter out that gorgeous view I loved...and keep crawling—and sometimes running—feet in. A wall that we could open and close as we chose.

At least until our mountain offspring was grown enough to know the lay of the literal land.

Walker swung in off the side of the mountain, flicking off the myriad of carabiner clips that hung from his belt attached to several ropes I made him put up for safety's sake. He objected, as did I.

My voice won out.

Or he let me win.

I preferred to go with option A. Either way, I felt more secure with him all strapped in when he worked on the impossible wall he seemed to build out of nothing, but then he knew this section of the mountain intimately. Dusty hands wrapped around me as I squeaked and batted at him but that didn't stop the Walker from nuzzling into the crook of my neck.

"Your beard is ticklish," I muttered, only half sassing him out.

"And you're fucking beautiful." He brushed his chin roughly against my cheek and claimed my mouth in a deep kiss. "When I'm finished later, we're sharing a warm pool. Then I'm showing you what that extra shallow area is made for."

His kisses grew deeper until I moaned, then he drew back. I flapped at him, but the glitter in Walker's eye told me I wasn't getting anything else from him until he was good and ready. Pouting, I let him lift me in his arms and place me in his rocker gently, wrapping me up in his thick blanket. The same one he had wrapped around me on the first night I invaded his home months ago.

Then he knelt and addressed my bump. Well, our bump, because we both made the little kicking bubble that grew inside. Our mountain blessing.

"Your mother might be sassy, but she's strong. You're gonna need that strength out here. But it's the most beautiful place in the world. She says it all the time when she thinks I'm not listening, but I am," he told my stomach.

I ran my fingers through Walker's hair where he was starting to let it grow out on top a little. "And your daddy is the craziest mo—"

Walker's hand rose to clamp over half my face. "Shh," he reprimanded me. "Potty mouth."

The glimmer in his eyes from before promised me filthy things for later. I looked forward to his demonstration of the shallow and warm pool he had spent the last few weeks carving out while I napped in the mountain's heart.

This place would always be ours, even when we lived closer to town. It wasn't just Walker's and it wasn't just the place where we met or where my car fell off the side and hadn't been recovered yet. Maybe one day. It was the place where I met a recluse of a mountain man who thought he'd been forgotten. But that had never been true.

No, this was a place that belonged to both of us. A place where we left our hearts in the secret sacred spaces within the mountain, our promise to return together.

Because together, we would never forget each other.

WHISPERED ECHOES
SERIES TWO

FORSAKEN
MOUNTAIN MAN

USA TODAY BEST SELLING AUTHOR
SOFIA AVES

I left the world behind a long time ago. The woman I thought I loved showed me what heartbreak is like. I knew then that I could do a whole lot better on my own.

So I walked away.

Everything. Everyone.

Picked up my work, my trade, and walked the f*ck away.

Until *she* decides that it's time for me to show my face again. Not that I know her, though she knows me.

My work. My art.

And it's enough for her to risk everything for a man she's never met.

Last time I gave my trust, it hurt. I still bear those scars.

Now she needs something I'm not sure I can give someone perfect like her. Hell, I'm not sure I should.

But she makes me want to try.

CHAPTER ONE

CORA

Three days after I left Red Hart Ranch and headed into the rugged mountains behind the big house, I found Bode Hunter's cabin.

I hadn't planned on tackling the entire hike to the estranged artisan gem carver's hut quite so quickly, but the weather closed in on me during day one, so I made tracks to avoid getting soggier than a wet wolf in springtime. Tracks I sloshed about on the rough and ready not-trail that I forged myself, because apparently I managed to lose the one both Travis and Trader Kyle mentioned could disappear on me at a moment's notice.

That didn't stop me from heading in the direction of my ultimate destination: the remote, reclusive man who carved Red Hart's Yogo sapphires by hand into intricate works of art. The man who I needed to convince to sell his wares to the only nearby jewelry store: White Cap's *Gem on the Range* where I'd worked for the past three years, sourcing some of the most unique jewelry and suppliers in northern Montana.

White Cap sat a good few hours from Red Hart Ranch, run by a pair of twins, Travis and Eve. Bode Hunter's cabin was... well, *three days' walk* was the most accurate gauge I had after that, because with no path and a mud map in hand plus no vehicle access in sight, there wasn't any other way I could describe the mountain man's choice of living situation.

Except maybe beautiful.

Rugged. Remote.

These trees I walked beneath only saw attrition from their fellows or in a storm. No roads or other damage felled their thick trunks out here, apart from the small clearing around Bode Hunter's rustic, hand built hut.

And for the last few days, I'd wondered what on earth had happened to this man that made him want to walk away from the rest of humanity, leaving society so far behind that he refused to come back, and exist alone out here.

Not that I truly questioned his life choices. I mean, the man was an artist and, from trader Kyle's samples spread over the twins' table back at the Red Hart big house, Bode obviously had talent and inspiration aplenty out here. His carvings of their rough stones were incredible. Animals, plants, leaves, flowers. Every aspect was captured in lifelike, stunning detail. I could see those carvings fitted into fine gold pieces that would be heirloom keepsakes passed down for generations.

That was the level of skill the man who I hunted —ha, pun intended—today, possessed. And I'd walked all the way out here to locate him. Having found his house, I considered the job fifty percent complete. But the yard was empty and no smoke rose from the chimney, considering the chill in the air at this altitude with the whisper of winter's tendrils in the air.

I should know. I didn't stop walking for the first day in an effort to dry the only clothes I brought with me—the ones on my back that started drenched in the sudden deluge the moment I passed the only other hut out here. That one belonged to Walker Roan. But he was busy building, or

rebuilding, his mountain view home to accommo-
date a growing family of his own. I had no intention
of interrupting his slice of peace.

And so I powered on to end up here.

Alone.

My intended destination.

"Hello, the house," I called, not wanting to inter-
rupt the man in his private space or scare him.

Maybe he was as soft and quiet as his art
suggested? Trader Kyle had gifted me a carved
bitterroot bloom, its petals curved so slightly that I
swore the entire bud would fold in my fingers the
moment I closed my hand, and disappear before I
opened it again, such was Bode Hunter's skill. I'd
opened my fingers on more than one occasion to
check it still existed and hadn't crumbled away
while I wasn't looking.

I stopped walking, though I rubbed my thumb
over the gem's center more than once, for luck. The
stone seemed to warm between my fingers just
before I slipped it back into my pocket.

My mouth opened, but I didn't call out again.
The yard's sense of stillness left me in a quiet mode I
wasn't used to after seventy-two hours and change
of constant motion with little sleep. My nerves
buzzed beneath my skin with the need to complete

my mission before I crashed out and headed back, but I had to face it: the house appeared deserted.

Even the birds had stopped singing.

The implications of that thought caught up with me way too late, along with the crack at my back.

I squeezed my eyes shut, already muttering under my breath. "Seriously, now?" I pivoted slowly on my heel, hands half raised. I hoped it was the right sort of bear to get myself big for, and not the death dealing sort.

Or a not-bear, at all. Yes. Not-a-bear would be a whole lot better right now.

My circle completed, I found myself peering at a dark, hair covered face with matching dark eyes. The beast who stared down at me from a towering height growled, too. I wondered if I should answer in kind, then decided against it as folly.

Because this particular beast held a rifle with the wrong end pointed at me so close I swore I could see his eye through the other end of the scope.

Not true, but the comical impression left me giggling at an inopportune moment.

My not-a-bear man stared me down a second longer, then lowered his weapon.

"What the hell are you doing on my land?" he groused, still glaring at me.

Maybe the artisan wasn't a soft man after all. But at least I'd completed my mission. Good thing, because my legs were ready to give out and I could do with that sleep now that I'd missed for the past few days. I managed a wan smile as I stumbled backward, all too aware of his muttered curses as he discarded the rifle and lunged forward to catch me as I dropped.

Yep, I could sleep now. And I didn't have to battle a bear. Win-win really, because I'd achieved my aim.

I'd found Bode Hunter.

CHAPTER TWO

BODE

I stared at the slip of a woman who looked like she'd been through hell to get up my mountain. After the first sentence I spat at her, words failed me. Not uncommon; I wasn't used to talking, period. Part of the reason I came out here in the first place was that I didn't like the company of others.

Which still begged the question, what was she doing on my front lawn.

If my lawn was full of dust, granite, and she was dressed in clothes that looked like she'd been caught in a cloudburst then slept in them for the past few days between Red Hart to here, however long that took her.

Hell, considering the tiny backpack she carried, they probably *were* the same clothes she started out in.

Not a stupid strategy, as long as that was what she expected. The way she stared back at me, thirty percent exasperation and seventy percent curiosity from the safety of my arms as she came around after half tumbling to the ground from what looked like either pure exhaustion, sunstroke, or a mix of both, maybe it was. But when she dropped in front of me, her thin legs beneath bottle green cargos covered in patches of grit, I tossed aside the barriers I'd erected as a last-ditch effort to keep the world out, and launched forward in a display of the training banged into me so long ago.

Because once, I'd worn a uniform and served. But that was a different life, back when there'd been someone worth coming home to. Someone worth returning from deployment *for*, before that same someone took every inch of my trust and shattered it.

And here we were.

A different girl I didn't know curled in my arms, staring up at me like I was a fascination she couldn't decipher.

Right back atcha, sprite.

"You are not what I expected, Bode Hunter." She said my first name in a stilted way, pronouncing it Bow-d, without the extended 'eee' sound at the end.

Whatever. I'd forgive her for mangling my name in a second, if I could stare into those deep brown eyes that matched her dark chocolate hair a while longer.

Then the penny dropped.

"What the fuck."

I placed my not-random hiker who knew my name gently back on her feet, hoping she would stay upright on her own. Still cursing and muttering on a fast rasping throat, I grabbed for my rifle, glad the damn thing hadn't discharged when I threw it before, and backed the hell up.

This was no random incursion, and no random girl.

"You're not what I expected for an artist," she offered, a soft smile gentling her already pretty face.

I raked trembling fingers through my hair. "Christ, no one's supposed to come out here." I coughed on the excess chatter, already choking on the thought of small talk. I didn't want anyone in my yard, let alone this stunning woman. She looked like she needed medical attention then a firm hand to turn her tidy behind about and get her off my mountain. "Get inside and have some water. Then you're going back where you came from."

"Mmm." She made a quiet sound that might have been agreement or discontent.

Either way, that hum went straight to my cock.

Shaking my head, I led her out of the heat and under the porch. "Leave your things there." I pointed to the utilitarian bench that dipped at one end that I used each morning and evening to get my boots on. "Come in and clean up. Then you're gone again. Understand?"

She didn't make a sound.

I swung about to check she hadn't passed out on me again, and found her right behind me. Her shoes were off in the place where mine usually sat, but her bag was clutched tight in her arms. At least it was off her back.

"Where it goes, I go." She stared up at me defiantly. A dare behind her eyes challenged me to defy her.

I didn't have the energy to play combat games right now. "Sure, sprite. Make yourself at home." To my surprise, the corner of my mouth quirked upward as I motioned her in front of me through the open door.

She murmured her thanks and that same instant arousal spike hit me a second time.

She's gotta go.

But damn if I didn't like the fact that someone—even a tiny woman encrusted with half the mountain's dirt with a big attitude problem—could make me smile.

I cleared my throat as she found my wooden table at one end of my living space and set her things on the floor beside it. "You know my name, but I don't know why–"

"I came out here to talk to you." She ignored my intent and rummaged through her things, head down, ass in the air.

I got an eyeful of curves as she faced the wrong direction, or maybe the right one, digging through her pack. A few expired rations pouches I recognized were laid out in haphazard piles.

Crouching nearby, but not too close, I collected her rubbish. "You got these from Travis down at the ranch."

She nodded, or at least, her hair did as she continued rummaging without raising her head. "Yep. He sorted me out when I came through Red

Hart a few days back. Him and trader Kyle. Freaking love Kyle. He's been amazing."

Another name's name on her lips sent a jolt through my chest. I crumpled her rubbish into my fist and removed it to the bin system at the back of my kitchen.

"Thank you," she called. "That leaves me more space for the return trip."

"Which will be soon," I muttered under my breath. "I'll top you up before you go." I wasn't that cruel, but I also wasn't used to talking. My breath and voice officially expired on that last word. I pulled out a chair from my table for her, and one on the corner for me. When she didn't notice, I reached across and grabbed a hip, squeezing. "Sit."

Mistake.

Touching her was the worst thing I could do. Despite her skin and bones appearance, my fingers sank into her flesh to that *just right* point. The point where I could pull her back into me, and—

Fuck.

I let her go as she gasped at the contact. "Sit," I growled. The single sound ripped my throat.

My voice was done, along with my sense of peace. Whoever she thought she'd come out here to see had died a long time ago.

Bode Hunter wasn't the same man who walked into these hills and built a house near on a decade ago. That man with the broken heart, he used to care. I lost that sense of humanity a long time ago. Travis and Kyle should have warned her about me. Shit, maybe they had. Maybe she'd been too gung ho about whatever she'd gotten into her head that brought her up here and nothing they said would have stopped her.

"Thank you." Her quiet answer blew my mind.

While I was ranting inside my head, she was off being all sweet and gentle. Christ, I wasn't fit company for a woman like her. Maybe I never had been.

"You shouldn't be here. Not with someone like me." The words came out so faded and thin, I wasn't sure she'd heard them. Not until she straightened up and scattered a handful of stones across the table. Stones that I recognized because I'd spent the last years carving them. Her eyes flashed with triumph as she tossed her hair in an undeniable *ta-daa* gesture.

No, not stones. At least not the sort you pick up from the ground. No, these came out of a river. At least, they did around here. Red Hart's river. Because these were Yogo sapphires, and they originated from the mountain right behind Red Hart Ranch.

I stared at the carved gemstones, recognizing my own art. "Fucking Kyle."

She grinned at me, those damn pretty eyes sparkling with the sort of mischief I wanted to hate but couldn't. "He's good, isn't he?" she agreed.

She. Because while *she* knew my name, I didn't know hers.

"Alright, sprite. Tell me why you're here. And start with your name." I coughed into my hand, pushing my chair back, needing the distance from her.

She nodded. "I'm gonna get myself that water first," she told me. "And wash up. Alright?"

I blinked and nodded, waving her in the direction of the other rooms in my cabin. It wasn't like she could get lost.

She wandered away from the table, running her fingertips along my shelves, padding barefoot through my house.

Releasing a slow breath, I leaned back and watched her. Maybe it wasn't so bad having a girl back in my house. Maybe I could deal with someone else in my space, even if she challenged everything about me in the few seconds she'd been here.

Maybe I'd let her stay a little longer and find out what she wanted. Work out why Kyle sent her in my direction.

My sprite disappeared along the darkened hallway that ran through the middle of the house like a vein through the mountain before I realized she'd left without giving me what I'd asked for.

I still didn't know her damn name.

CHAPTER THREE

CORA

Bode Hunter's home smelled of crisp air and pine, as though he had brought the mountain inside along with him. I wandered along the dimly lit hall, having found myself a decent glass of water and the bathroom, thankfully. His house was longer than it appeared from the outside, not the short, squat little building it seemed from the front at all, but lancing back into the cliff face. One wall consisted entirely of granite, leading the length of the hallway and deeper into his home.

That was the path I followed, trailing my fingers along its rough surface as I walked, half expecting to drop off the side of a never ending ledge at any moment. I knew I was being nosy, poking around his house, but I'd walked for three days to get here, been soaked to the skin, dried again, and rolled in dirt when I slipped down a small incline. Yes, I was curious about the man I'd been sent to negotiate with. No part of me felt the least part guilty about learning more about him with every step deeper into his home.

Doorways on the other side of the hallway led to rooms that appeared unused. Spare bedrooms, another bathroom. The entire place was fitted out for a much bigger family as though he had expected it to be filled by people who never arrived.

Or maybe someone who left.

My heart clenched at the thought as I discovered the final room along the hall where the house stopped at a dead end. Here, the walls were all rock, the last room hewn into the side of the mountain altogether. I peered through the granite arch with no door, knowing I shouldn't. This was his private space, right at the other end of the house. I knew that, but I did it anyway.

Because I wanted to know what sort of a man Bode Hunter was.

And when I stared into his bedroom, I saw... Mountains.

Literal, huge, mountains that stretched on and on through a valley that should rightfully be called a ravine. Each violently dipped side was covered with conifers and steep, unforgiving rockfaces. Above, the edges were tall enough to be ringed with wispy clouds and tipped at the apex with snow caps. I shivered just looking at the vista laid out before me.

It was all too easy to imagine the wind whistling through the cleft in the world that I swore some deity had sliced a finger through the earth's surface and scraped half of it away.

All this viewed through a giant piece of glass that should never have been possible to haul this far out. Actually, with his strange skill set, I wondered if my artisan hadn't made it. A bed perched on a hard-wood floor, the same color as the frame, and I knew he *had* made that.

Little else sat in his room, personalising it. Apparently, Bode's inner sanctum was as spartan as the man who protected it. I hadn't been wrong about my initial assessment of him. Now to get back before he realized I'd gotten 'lost' in his one-hallway house and came looking for me.

The concept slapped me with a mini deadline. I

blinked and took a step back, right into a warm wall blocking my retreat that I swore hadn't been there before. A fresh wash of cold mountain air draped over me.

I swear this man is an obscure deity drawn from the centre of this place itself.

I pivoted around, already knowing what—or who—I'd find as I backed deeper into Bode's room, facing the man himself.

"Couldn't you find the bathroom?" he drawled softly. His voice rasped, as though the short conversation earlier had zapped his vocal strength.

Who knew? It probably had. I doubted he did much in terms of conversation up here, unless it was with the local bear. I figured that was what he decided to take a shot at when I came walking into his personal space.

"Uh huh. Yep. Found the bathroom," I said brightly. "Then got turned about on my way back to the kitchen. Living area." I peered around him hopefully and pointed. "That way?"

I mean, it was the only way back from here. It wasn't like I could really get lost. We both knew that.

"Yep. That way." Bode repeated softly. Dark cobalt eyes narrowed as I sidled past him, sucking in my tummy since he didn't help the situation at all by being the literal bear blocking the doorway.

"Oh, look. Found it." I maintained my cheerful tone as I sauntered away from him, relieved of my new found freedom. Maybe snooping around his house uninvited hadn't been my best idea. But now I had a clearer plan of how I wanted this afternoon to progress, so I had drawn some inspiration from my investigation of Bode Hunter, on top of what Kyle told me back at Red Hart.

A hand clamped down on my wrist halted my progress and stole the breath from my lungs. A not so courageous squeak evicted from my mouth.

"Maybe you should be careful of what you look for out here. It's not the same as civilization on the range, Cora Welk."

I stared at him for a long moment, then my stare became a frown. "You went through my things."

He inclined his head, neither denying my accusation, nor letting my wrist go. Tiny tingles raced along my bare skin where his rough fingers gripped my arm. "You went through my things. I returned the favor," he said evenly.

My lips curved into a smile. "Fair enough." I matched his tone. "I came up here to do a job, Mister Hunter. Are you ready to negotiate?"

His fingers flexed enough on my arm for me to slide my wrist free of his grip. I continued my walk along the hall, conscious of his gaze on my back the entire way.

If this was what Bode was like now, what would he say when I asked to buy half his art?

CHAPTER FOUR

BODE

"No."

I stared at the pretty little sprite seated across the table from me. My gaze flickered down to the portfolio that displayed pictures of nearly every carving I'd ever sold to Trader Kyle over the past ten years, and back to her determined, chocolate eyes.

Fuck, she was too pretty for this. Maybe that was why her boss sent her up my mountain. He sure as fuck knew what he was doing. A girl who could survive the walk in, negotiate like she just did and look at me as pretty as that across the table?

I had one word for Cora Welk:

Bait.

"No." I repeated the single syllable when she didn't so much as react. Pushing my chair back, still staring at her, because I couldn't take my eyes off the way her lips curled when I denied her, I itched to see what she looked like when she really smiled. "No."

"I want you to say it again."

Cora—dammit, I couldn't get enough of her name on my tongue, even if I wasn't saying it— leaned forward. Her arms crossed beneath her breasts under her singlet top that clung to every curve. I'd been right; what she wore hiking were the only clothes she'd brought with her.

Fuck, if she hadn't been sexy as all get out before, then that sealed the deal. The girl before me was tough as hell, and damn intelligent on top of all that.

Everything I wanted in a woman.

I should have turned her around and sent her on her way an hour ago, despite that the unseasonal cloud burst heralded worse weather on its way and fast. So why was she still sitting at my table, and why was I entertaining the idea of giving her every- thing she wanted?

Cora's eyes sparkled like she knew she had me, and fuck if I didn't lean back in my chair, waiting for her to sell me what the hell ever she came all the way out here to say.

Again.

Because we'd been around this bear trap a few times already. But saying *no* to this woman was just a warm up for her, it seemed. I swallowed back a mouthful of scalding black coffee and waited.

"I want your art. The shop where I work in White Cap would like your art. But, Bode," she pronounced my name correctly this time. I'd fixed that after my third *no*. And she still hadn't backed down. My respect grew for the woman who both irritated me and blew me away with every word. "Seriously, these pieces never last more than a few days in their glass cases. I've been selling your pieces for years. We should be collecting them in a gallery. You have no idea."

I frowned at her. That was taking it a bit far. Sure, I got that the gems were stunning, and I appreciated that someone else liked my version of art. That actually felt good for about half a second before I quashed the idea with a solid bout of imposter syndrome. Hell, it was part of the reason I chose a bank of mountains between me and the rest of the world.

Walker Roan got that, the man who helped me

build this place around the curve in the mountainside when I first walked past his cabin set back in the mountain behind Red Hart Ranch years ago. He helped me drag tools out once I'd settled on a place and drew up the contract with Len Beaumont. That was back when the old man was still the owner of Red Hart, before his son, Travis, took over. And Eve. Another spitfire of a woman, though I'd heard she had her own Ranger to tame.

"I'm not putting anything in a gallery," I said tersely, drawing my attention back to Cora and the problem she presented to my present. Namely, that she was in my house, asking for something I didn't want to give her.

But why not?

"That's four." She drained her mug and rose, managing not to scrape her chair on the granite floor that formed half my mountain. "Would you like a top up?"

"You're not leaving?" I wasn't sure if I wanted her to go, or was impressed by her tenacity to stay despite my not so subtle hints to the contrary.

Cora's laugh filled my kitchen as she liberated my mug and sashayed across my house. "No, Bode Hunter. I'm not leaving until you agree to let me stock some of your carvings. Or everything that you have." She shrugged, her back to me as she refilled her mug and mine with my shitty, stale instant coffee that was likely several years out of date. Not a single word of complaint from this woman, though. Unlike—

I cleared my throat in an attempt to dispel the old memories that still haunted me whenever I allowed them in. "And if I refuse to give you anything to stock from here on in?"

Fucking Kyle. I hadn't figured the trader was selling my art to anyone other than a few ranches or families. I'd have a few words with the younger man with a silver tongue the next time I saw him, though I suspected he'd make himself scarce in the coming months.

"You won't."

Cora returned to the table with a pair of matching, steaming mugs. I stared at them, unable to remember the last time I sat with a woman to talk, shared a cup of coffee with her.

Lie.

That memory shattered in a swirl of steam that rose between us, obscuring Cora's pretty face. Suddenly, it was all too close, the years I'd been here too few.

My teeth ground together as I shoved my chair

back at the same time as Cora sat her perfectly proportioned tush down in a chair that I'd made from scratch myself.

"Take all the time you need," she murmured, flicking through the portfolio I suspected she had put together from some of my earliest work.

If that wasn't a long term fan, then I had no idea how else to categorize her.

Pretty, stunning...hypnotic.

I opted to ignore the woman seated at my table, my chest constricting with a significant lack of air as I headed for the door to the cabin that was too small for two people. The mountain's weight bore over me. The door jammed as I shoved at it. Fuck it, was everything going to break on cue? My boot hit the soft wood on the way out, leaving a fresh dent in the far corner. I swore prolifically at the mark, the door and the woman who had invaded my space.

Cora Welk had no right being out here, away from everything that she knew. Not on my mountain, talking about my art, or near me.

And damn well not being as tough, sassy or as pretty as she was in my living space, not complaining about a damn thing or accepting me as I was. Dammit, she was too fucking perfect, and I wasn't fit to breathe the same air as she did for a second more.

I strode down the goat track that circled around the side of the cabin, knowing she'd never find it, and headed as far away from Cora Walk as I could. Hopefully, by the time my head cleared and I returned to the house, she'd have given up and left. And I'd be alone, just like I always planned.

So why did that seem like such a bad idea?

My footfalls reverberated off the mountainside as I stormed deeper into the valley heading for a place I knew would settle the rage inside me. And prayed I'd be wrong when I returned later.

Or not.

CHAPTER FIVE

CORA

I waited exactly three minutes before I followed Bode outside his home. *Take all the time you need* was a frame of reference statement, and mine expired with the dregs of my second cup of black coffee.

Mind, I needed that coffee just to stay awake. Negotiating with a block of granite—essentially my job for the day as Bode could be defined as *unyielding, unfathomable* and *fixed point* all at once.

When Bode left the house, he turned a sharp right. Somehow, I suspected that he thought I wouldn't find the thin track well-worn deep into the mountainside, its entrance hidden beneath a stand of Rocky Mountain Juniper clustered tightly together. He'd snapped a few wayward twigs on his way through, leaving the path clear to me. I sidled between the damaged branches, the sharp cedar-like notes blooming in the crisp air.

I swear this man is a mountain personified. Shaking the thought away I pushed between the shrubby trees, careful not to dislodge a few older bird's nests higher up, waiting on their owners' to return next season, maybe. I could imagine what Bode's home must be like in springtime, teeming with life. Newborns, chirping birds. Maybe a few fawns.

Smiling at the image of the enormous mountain man surrounded by wildlife like a mountain version of Snow White, I made my way along the narrow track cut into the side of the granite, hugging the rock face as best I could. Bode might be used to the instant-death drop on one side, but the idea of plummeting to my fate, albeit a stunning one, wasn't in my book for today.

A chill wind brushed my bare shoulders. Goose-flesh erupted over my skin beneath my singlet as I continued into the shadows. How Bode made it down the ledge-like path without falling off the edge of the world, I had no idea. The air chilled as I made my way downward, winding across the steep rock face that curved inward. A rushing sound reached me. I wrapped my arms tighter around myself as the granite track thankfully widened out.

Without the constant threat of imminent death from slippage as my fate, I continued on at a slightly faster pace. Another curve, and I swore I'd stare at the inside of the mountain. Instead, I discovered the rushing sound. It wasn't wind, like I'd thought, but I had found the source of what chilled the air, apart from the breeze rushing through the valley to batter the rock face.

Water droplets splashed me, hanging suspended in the semi-saturated air as I stared into the great cavern partially lit with sunlight that filtered through from a great cathedral ceiling high above.

Almost as high, I guessed, as the base of Bode's house.

And at the bottom of the cavern sat a pool, though the water wasn't still. A tall waterfall disturbed its serenity, and beneath its tumbling, endless spray stood the man I sought. Bode's back faced me, his chin upturned beneath the force of the unyielding element, almost as unforgiving as the man himself.

"This is where you hide," I whispered to myself, unable to take my eyes off the naked back presented to me. Where Bode took himself away from the world when even exposure on the mountain's stark face grew too much. And then I knew that before, I hadn't been wrong, but I was now. If exploring Bode's house had been an invasion of his privacy, then this was something else altogether. "I shouldn't be here."

I retreated a step, my feet skittering on the path in my haste.

Bode, with his sense of impossibility attuned to everything in this place as remote and unattainable and as forsaken as the mountain man himself, turned beneath the water's force. His eyes opened as he stared up at me, unflinching, almost as though he had expected me to be here.

Which was impossible, a second time over, as I hadn't known I'd be here myself. Or had I always known I'd follow him? My feet retreated another step before I could think the motion through.

Bode raised a hand, curling his fingers inward.

Come here.

He didn't repeat the gesture before he lowered his hand, still standing beneath the water. Those fathomless eyes closed, leaving me alone on the ledge.

Letting me make my own decisions.

I stood, watching him. Water sluiced over heavy

arms and a thick torso rippled with more muscle than I knew what to do with. Out here, all that was hard earned and I had no doubt that every part of him was much needed for pure survival. Except maybe that smattering of dark hair across his chest that wound in a fine trail much lower. The water obscured everything below in a haze of white.

Without opening his eyes, Bode stepped forward, out of the spray, as though knowing I needed to continue my perusal of him.

And ...There was a reason this man stayed within the mountains. Because mere mortal men could not stand up next to him.

Shame on them.

Thick thighs were the perfectly proportioned home for the length that hung between them. Bode could walk for days without stopping for the look of him and what he could do with *other parts*...

I rolled my lips inward, willing the insta-fantasies back, then decided not to bother.

Because my feet took those next steps forward on their own.

What a liar I am. I took those steps consciously.

As long as that trek down his mountainside had seemed from his home to the ledge and to here, the next took no time at all. I stood before him in my filthy, three day old clothes drenched with the residual spray where Bode had emerged from the water to meet me. He still appeared as some sort of archaic mountain god drawn from an unknown realm, drifting toward his chosen mortal.

How fanciful could I possibly be?

But this was the man who drew wildlife and flora from literal gemstones, extracting their faces from perfect stones themselves. And now he stood before me, rivulets of pristine mountain water running over musculature that appeared as though he, too, had been carved from the earth's stone.

The way he called to me, curling his fingers... I shivered. My body's response had nothing to do with the plummeting temperature in the caves, away from the few shafts of sunlight that filtered in from above, though that same pale warmth didn't make it to where he stood beneath the water's fall.

"I shouldn't have come down here." My apology tumbled from my lips, the first thought that fell out of my mouth the moment I opened it.

"Yet here you are." Bode watched me through heavy eyes. His shoulders were more relaxed than they had been in the cabin above us.

"I followed you." All the unnecessary words I

uttered, my pithy volume stripped away by the cacophony that surrounded us.

He didn't seem bothered by the constant white noise that I couldn't block out. Those same damned fingers raised, curling inwards.

"What? No." I wrapped my hands around my midsection in a one person hug, getting the joke. His sense of humor was as wacky as my own. He'd finally turned the tables on me. Up at the surface level, in his living area, he'd been the one saying *no*. How neatly Bode Hunter had reversed our positions. Still, I had my own objections to this situation. "I'm not suicidal, thank you. It's freezing."

Bode's expression never changed, but I swore his lips flickered in the faintest semblance of a smile before he sank back beneath the wall of water, the constant spray obscuring him from sight.

"Bode?" I stared at him, or where he had been, nonplussed. Was he coming back out? Was I supposed to leave? His invitation only seemed to extend so far, and my feet were already wet.

This is insane. I just met this man.

But he was everything that seemed perfect about this place. I had walked for three days through mountains and rain storms to meet Bode Hunter. What the hell was the point of being here if I didn't understand the real man who made such stunning art if I turned down an opportunity like this?

Yeah, because that's the real reason you want to go waterfall swimming with a man you just met who tried to kick you out of his house but couldn't because you were too stubborn about a job you obsess over.

Not that any of that mattered right now.

My decision made for me, I stepped through the veil of water, and into his world.

CHAPTER SIX

CORA

Silence cocooned around me in a cold sluice. The interruption of static and chatter, even within my own head, lasted a full second, nothing more. Bode's hand, unseen, wrapped around mine, pulling me deeper. I crashed against his chest, my body pressed flush to his.

If I thought I'd been drenched before, I had nothing on right now. Every inch of my clothing was wet through to the inner parts. A violent tremor wracked me as Bode Hunter gazed down with those same unchanging eyes that brooked no argument. Even so, I had the sense that he was pleased I stood before him.

Heat from his oversized body eked into mine, whittling away like the water that washed over us, cleansing in its endless downpour. Neither of us spoke. I didn't think we'd be able to hear one another beneath the endless roar, or end up drinking everything above us. Still, he leaned down and rested his forehead gently against mine.

Warmth seared me at every point of contact: where his brow touched mine, where our noses grazed. Thighs grazing, bellies pressed together. Our fingers brushed as I swayed on the spot, though he stood still, unmovable as the mountain itself.

Bode's hands wrapped around mine, warm and secure anchors in a deluge of overwhelm.

You're safe here.

Let go.

So I did.

When he tugged the drenched hem of my single top upward, baring my stomach without breaking our locked gaze, I let him. He peeled the material over my body with exquisite care, but never pulled back. If we had been anywhere else, I knew his breath would have brushed over my skin, but here, the water washed it away before I could feel its heat, stealing that first, intimate kiss.

His lips never contacted mine. Not when he

reached around to unhook my bra, running his fingers under the straps that had added to my skin with sweat and sunscreen, or where he traced over my ribs and along my sides as icy mountain water cascaded over my breasts, washing away days of hiking, the pilgrimage I'd undertaken to reach him, baptising me in his own way.

Callused thumbs traced patterns across my hips as they worked their way forward. His touch never rushed as he found the button at the front of my cargos, worked the zip there. Bode peeled those down too, pushing until the tight material gave enough to puddle at my feet.

Most of the time I forgot to breathe, sucking in chill air enough to keep my mind from fritzing out, my eyes locked on his dark gaze that never wavered. This man was intoxicating, his attention hypnotic. I couldn't walk away from him if I tried, and I swore breathing near him was actually optional.

Strong, rough hands closed around my hips. He lifted me off my feet. My wet clothing dropped away, leaving me only in my panties which had long passed their usefulness. I flicked at the sides but as he slid me along his body, one hand gripped the back and *tore*.

The single, violent motion left me without

thought. Without anything useful as Bode's mouth finally came down hard on mine and obscured everything.

The world, the cavern. The water.

All that existed was him.

And I fell.

That was okay, because he caught me. Held me to him in a firm embrace as his mouth pressed mine open, enough for his tongue to swipe across my bottom lip, seeking entry. My moan—of need, desperation, everything building and building to a crescendo I wasn't sure I could match—sank between us into a pocket of air scented like him that I drowned in.

Bode never let me go through his slow, deep kisses. His fingers gripped mine, wrapping them around his granite length. I whimpered into his mouth, salivating at the size of him. Everything about him was in perfect proportion. Huge, and impossible but perfect all the same. I stroked him, letting his warmth fill my hands, getting used to the size of him.

Heat bloomed between my legs, a burn that not even the icy deluge could extinguish. He held me close, not letting the tumbling drops sweep me away. Not even when my knees dipped, intent as I was on worshipping him with my mouth. I needed his hands pulling at my hair as he guided me, taught me to please him, the bruises I'd earn on my knees. My mewl became a frustrated sound he smothered with his tongue thrust deep.

Fluid gushed low and hot between my thighs as he lifted me instead right over him. My sounds mingled with his growl as he seated me over his length, notched at my soaked entrance. One fist wrapped around himself, he worked his cockhead there, teasing us both as I wriggled in place for him, panting into his mouth until no breath remained. My nails scored new tattoos over his skin as he moved with me, finding a teasing rhythm as I worked myself into a frenzy—

And he dropped me onto his length, letting my weight and dripping need impale myself on the top of his thick length.

My scream reverberated around the cavern. Pleasure and shock bounced back at me, my own voice fractured into a thousand different versions of myself as Bode pushed me deeper onto his cock. I stretched around him, taking what he needed from me with little resistance, aided by the gush he'd created with his deep kisses earlier.

His mouth clamped back over mine, stealing

every sound from then until the only ones left were the fading echoes of my first cry as I sank to the root of him, muscles fluttering and clamping at the invading presence that I needed more than the breath he wouldn't let me take.

The hands gripping my hips squeezed as he leaned back, bracing my weight. Then Bode *moved*.

Nothing like his slower kisses from before. This was the violent man who tore my panties from my legs minutes ago with zero hesitation. His hold tightened as he railed into me. Cords stood out on his neck, arms braced as tight as his legs beneath us. Everything I saw was viewed through a distant haze the moment he withdrew to slam back home in a flurry of movement that left me aching. Pleasure tore through me in an overwhelm of everything far too sensitive to absorb. Suddenly, the needle sharp icy water droplets were the softest points of contact about our chosen environment.

A wail built in me, but Bode was ready, crushing our mouths together, determined to secrete away every sound I made after letting that first scream rip free. I came on his cock, coating his tongue and his cock with my bliss at the same time. Thick arms banded around me, crushing me to his chest as he refused to let up, powering through my orgasm. I tried to kiss him back but I couldn't focus on anything. One wave of insanity rolled into the next and it was all I could do to cling to his slippery shoulders and not fall off the edge of existence.

Finally, I succumbed to what he wanted: hold onto him, let him kiss me and fuck me the way he desired and just...

Let go.

Fall.

Finally, I got it.

I stopped fighting against what he did, stopped trying to push and. *Let. Him. Fuck. Me.*

Bode growled low, the deep sound originating in his chest. The rumble darkened, like thunderheads in the valley beyond, and I swore the mountain reverberated with the sound. I clung to him, trusting him to hold us up as he roared my name. My mountain man slammed hilt deep as he came, flooding my insides with warmth.

My eyes drifted shut as I rested my cheek against the hollow of his shoulder, tasting fresh mountain water and salt where the mix of his flavours swirled across my cheeks and onto my tongue. I drank him in, lapping at his skin as he panted, crushing me to his body.

Bode lifted my chin in a firm grip, tipping my

head back as he walked us backward, out of the water. My butt planted on smooth rock still inside the spray, away from the falling water, facing the falls when I managed to crack my eyes open.

He never spoke as he laid me back onto the smoothed rock. I stared up at the cataclysm as he parted my legs on the curved rock ledge, the granite worn away by who knew how many days and years of the spray flowing over its hard surface to gentle the edges.

I sighed, letting him nestle between my legs, jerking when his tongue, hot compared to the water's cold kiss, touched my battered folds. I slammed my hand over my mouth, knowing he craved my silence now, in this place.

His altar of serenity.

I sank my teeth into my knuckles as Bode lapped at my drenched cunt, licking both of our fluids from my flesh. His hands kept my legs apart as he worked, sucking and cleaning, until I gushed for him fresh and hot and needy. Then his growls began again. His beard rubbed against tender flesh as I writhed, but he braced strong forearms over my thighs, holding me flat in place. I moaned into my cupped hands, biting my knuckles when his tongue grazed over my swollen clit, leaving me twitching and aching for more of him.

I mumbled at him behind my hands, begging and keeping my wishes to myself, but he made them all come true anyway. Bode sucked on my clit, gentle at first, then faster, flicking the tip of the tortured bud with a rough, too-fast rhythm until I screamed —loud and long and uncontrolled as I came for him.

Two fingers slammed deep inside me, fingers belonging to the man with the monster cock that stretched me before.

My body protested even as my pussy clamped down on him, sending fresh shock waves that refused to let my orgasm end. I rode the waves as he pumped his hand hard, my body bearing down on his palm. Sweat broke over my breasts, beading and dripping as I rolled my hips in time with his touch.

And the whole time he watched me, dark eyes intense and unyielding.

I came on a cry, having long given up trying to hide my pleasure from him or this place. Those fingers flicked deep inside me and I rode that new wave, too. Bode waited until my hips stopped jerking, and I stilled, panting. Then he climbed my body, straddling my face and slid a hand behind my head.

His cock pressed my lips, hard and engorged.

Exhausted but needy still, I pressed my sticky thighs together, lifting my head, grateful when he added his support, and sucked on the tip of his cock.

The velvet head with its hard, mushroom shape might be my favorite thing in the world. I could suck that all day when he stared down at me as he did, cobalt eyes hooded. One hand directed his cock down to me, the other massaged my nape as he held me in place so I wouldn't strain my neck. I opened my mouth, taking him deeper.

My body shook with the strain, but I wanted to please him. Again, he took my weight, lifting me with ease so I could swallow him. My legs parted as I squeezed his thighs, my empty pussy aching. One corner of his mouth quirked upward as though he knew what I needed. The hand gripping his cock let go, and he leaned back to reach between my legs, toying with me from the outside. Not penetrating me, but worse. So much worse. Just teasing, playing around the edges of my entrance, getting me nice and slick and messy.

I mewled, humping uselessly at his hand as he watched me pant and suck and lick at him, straining to take what I could of him from this angle, which wasn't much. But I did try to give him pleasure, bobbing my head and swirling my tongue around the swollen tip.

He growled when I flicked my tongue beneath the head and ran my lips along the underside. The hand playing with me disappeared to wrap back around his length. He leaned back a few inches to where I couldn't suck him anymore.

I frowned, missing the contact twice over as he worked his hand in a blur, his other still locked about the back of my neck. His fingers massaged there in languid circles, leaving me boneless and moaning. His breath came shorter, and he came on a low growl, ropes of white cum stringing across my breasts, painting my flesh and marking me as his.

I panted beneath him despite that he had done the work as he gazed down at me possessively. Thick fingers reached out to swirl through his cum, striping my breasts, teasing my nipples until I was a hot mess beneath him again. Then he brought his fingers to my lips as an offering.

I leaned forward, my body shivering with the simple strain, and sucked his fingers clean without thought.

"Beautiful, Cora. So perfect."

I smiled, leaning back onto the smooth rock, and closed my eyes.

Today had been perfect. Bode was right. Nothing what I ever expected, but perfect all the same.

Some indeterminable time later after he'd taken me again, slower this time, Bode scooped me into his arms and carried me back to the house. Not along the ledge that I'd walked down before, the one where I'd worried I would fall off the world from, but up a set of roughhewn stairs he'd cut into the inside of the mountain himself.

I didn't object at all, letting him hold me, our wet clothes bundled in my arms. Let him carry me to his shower, and experience hot water, then a hard but warm bed that also suited the man for both its density and its size. Both were also perfect, all the things I learned about Bode Hunter in this place.

The man who let me in, even when he told me he didn't want me to stay. The man who was so much more than the art he carved when that was all I'd hiked into his space for. So much more than just a job.

I curled against his chest that night, listened to the slow heartbeat of the mountain man who thought the world had forsaken him, but who had never been forgotten.

EPILOGUE

BODE

Three months after Cora Welk arrived in my life she was still here sitting at my table, working on drawings for her portfolio. And I figured her boss, or maybe Travis had worked out what happened, because no search party arrived to look for her even though the day after she found me beneath the waterfall in the cavern, the sky darkened and snow set in as winter arrived a full three weeks early.

That happened occasionally, with that strange onset of fall's last cloud burst as its final herald, as though the season decided to have its final fling across the mountainside. And then, the passes closed and we were snowbound for the foreseeable future.

Not that Cora seemed to mind simple mountain life at all. No more than I expected really when I saw her that first day, realized she had walked in with one set of clothes, a few rations in her bag, filthy, dirty in so many more ways than one, and refused to leave before she got her answer from me.

I wasn't sure if she ever got her answer, and she was still here.

But today, she didn't sit at my table alone. Because even though early winter still drifted across the mountain, the only person crazier than my nearest neighbor had come to visit, and I hadn't seen Walker Roan for a few months now, shut up in his own place a few mountains closer to Red Hart.

No, the visitor we had today made Cora very happy and changed the status quo that I'd adjusted to perfectly fine.

I just wasn't sure how this would play out...or if she'd stay after he'd had his say.

And so I sat at the other end of my table, drank fresh instant coffee Kyle gifted me—for a price, even though he hadn't disclosed what his was just yet—and said nothing at all.

"They miss you in White Cap." Kyle flipped idly

through the portfolio hosting my older designs and Cora's newer drawings of my newer works, seeing as I didn't have a printer. He spoke to both of us, but only she answered him.

"Maybe. Ben can get another sales girl. I'm staying." She leaned over and rested her head on my shoulder. "The jewelry shop was fun. Ten years of fun," she said much slower under Kyle's watchful gaze. "But also I think I'm here, now."

Kyle's eyes flicked up to meet mine. "Yeah?"

I held his gaze and didn't move. Didn't speak, either.

Sometimes, Kyle came up the range and spent a week talking to himself. I listened. Learned a lot, or learned nothing at all. At the end of the week we traded for what we both needed, and for what I felt was worth something to sell. Sometimes the trader walked around the house picking out things he wanted to buy.

Occasionally, he got to take them away with him.

He smiled when I didn't answer. "Sounds like a good place, then." He paused, and I knew he was loading his bait. Waited, because the younger nomadic trader was a master at his craft and everyone from White Cap to Red Hart and Black Hill to the properties beyond to the west knew that as well. "What about the Christmas trade? Or did you forget about that?"

Cora shifted beside me in a way that gave away her desire for something she wanted. "I—" She leaned away from me. I wrapped an arm around her waist, unwilling to let her move. She let me, but leaned forward, planting her elbows on the table. "I thought we had passed Christmas. Just...let it go." She looked back and shrugged. "I thought maybe you didn't celebrate it so I ignored dates once I got here. Kind of stopped counting and all."

I gifted her a faint smile that she returned with a much larger one. No words were necessary right there.

Kyle coughed. "It's in three weeks."

Okay, so maybe Cora had been with me for two months, and I couldn't count for shit. Wait– The penny dropped on a different realization. I frowned and tapped her thigh, ignoring Kyle. Her head angled sideways when I tapped her thigh again, a little harder.

She nodded. "I know."

"When?" My voice rasped from lack of use. Cora didn't make me talk, or talk when I asked for her silence. Utterly fucking prefect in all ways. I coughed, the sound dry, and seared my throat on the black coffee, seeking lubrication.

She knew. Of course she knew. It was her body. I should have known, too. But I'd been too damn loved up with her to focus on much else. And it had been a long time for me without a woman... Not that it should be any sort of excuse.

"When were you going to tell me?"

Cora shrugged. "Maybe next month? If I thought it was... real." Her cheeks heated on the lie.

I squeezed her waist in a silent promise.

A child. Here. For us. Fuck. I needed to be so much more for her. For all of us. But she wasn't backing down and... If this was what she wanted from me, then neither would I.

A woman walked out on me once before. I still had no idea what I didn't do to make the mark, only that it hurt enough that I hid myself away from the world when she broke my trust and another man took my place. This time, I promised Cora as I stared at her and ignored Kyle, I would be enough for all of us. Whatever she needed.

But there was the little matter that she hadn't told me. Something she needed to do as trust was a two way door.

We will talk about this later.

Even if *later* involved no words at all.

Kyle leaned back, letting us host our silent conversation until we were done, and then redirected us. "Ben needs the extra hand in the shop. White Cap gets busy during Christmas. If you need to go into town, we can travel together to Red Hart. One of the boys will give you a lift back in." He raised an eyebrow at me, clearly having followed the conversation.

"I miss the rush," she murmured, glancing at me, her brow dipping as she sought permission that she never needed to request from me. "Not the work, well, kind of. But Christmas is...it's busy. Crazy busy. Non-stop. And people are crazy. From the time you open, you're needed. You help all day, finding gifts, solving problems. It's...there's no other time of year like it." She glowed with every word. I knew what would come next.

I growled at Cora, and she giggled.

You shouldn't keep secrets from me, sprite.

No matter how long she'd been in the mountains with me or not, I still couldn't drop the name she'd earned on her first day here that seemed both yesterday and so long ago.

Without a word I shoved my chair back, emptied my coffee mug, dregs and all down my throat and strode for my bedroom. I had a duffle bag from my military days stowed somewhere. That would do for a few weeks' clothing and whatever else she would need.

Hell, Cora had been wearing my clothes with few alterations for the past months. Maybe when we came back she could bring some of her own things with her, set up what she wanted for the baby properly.

The plan spurred me on. I headed down the hallway until the silence in the living area brought me to a halt.

Kyle coughed, and Cora giggled.

"What are you doing?" she called.

I poked my head back out the hallway. "If you're keen on working Christmas each season, then we need to pack."

"We?" She stared at me, open mouthed.

I nodded, my throat already itchy from its long speech of thirteen words. "Yep, we. Going down the mountains. To Red Hart. And White Cap. All of us." I waved my finger in the air to include our unnamed mountain baby and Kyle, though I cast the trader a hard eye.

He just smiled and drank from my mug at my table while my girl giggled and grabbed her portfolio, already planning which of my carvings she'd take into town.

Guess I'd have a decent income to look after my new family each year if this was the plan from now on anyway. And if she wanted to do this each Christmas... Well, hell.

At least the trader might stay away a little more and I could get some quiet time with my girl once we came back home together.

All of us.

THANK YOU FOR READING

Thank you for reading Bode and Cora's story! Please do leave a review, even if it's a simple, 'I enjoyed reading this book!" or a star rating. It means a lot.
Truly.
Read other books in the WHISPERED ECHOES mountain man series season 2 here:
My Book

You can find Walker Roan in his own mountain man story in FORGOTTEN MOUNTAIN MAN and catch up all the RED HART RANCH cowboy romances with Travis, Eve, Kyle (yes, he gets his own HEA!) and the crew along the range.

READ ON

R ead on for a sneaky peek at MOUNTAIN MAN'S LOVE AT FROST SIGHT

SNEAKY PEEK: MOUNTAIN MAN'S LOVE AT FROST SIGHT

GABE

I haven't dealt with a single person in over four months, and that's the way I like it.

Hope Peak is the sort of small town in Montana that you can pass through on a tourist drive or stop and stay for a lifetime. It's the sort of small town that has secrets, a rumor mill that rivals any government agency in its efficiency, and a population so inbred that it keeps men like me away for most of the year.

I lie. There are no other men like me around my part of the town. Or more accurately, the part of the town that I'm farthest from.

Years ago, I took the advice of a ranger in that

same town after I came back from a desert mission and hiked into the mountains. After a week of messing around, I came back into town, found the land owner I needed to speak to and paid double what the little slice of peace that I found for myself was worth in order to keep the rest of the world at bay.

Which is why, when I stare through my rifle's scope and see the sort of mark that has nothing to do with my dinner but has the potential to sate a very different sort of appetite altogether, my interest sparks.

The woman in my mountains has no right to be here, and that makes her all the more fascinating.

Dressed in a dark green jacket that covers her to the knees but hangs open with a fluffy hood, I think she's a damn bear at first and nearly end her life before I have a chance to find out anything about her. But she's not a bear, or even a small bear, at that. The moment the flash of red of her checkered shirt, knotted at her navel to expose the swell of her stomach catches my eye, my focus shifts significantly. From there she's all curves of the luxurious sort. Not the hiker sort, that's for fucking sure. The sort a man can sink his hands into and—well. Do some damage. Her pale, tight jeans look painted on, and a fantasy of peeling them from her to find out how her flesh dimples beneath my roughened hands infiltrates my mind within seconds.

Hell, I'm an ex-soldier not a saint, for fuck's sake. And I never did get myself a Christmas present this season, Here's one ready made to order just for me.

Strawberry blonde hair is wound into a messy knot on top of her head, though plenty of strands escape around her face. Dirt streaks one cheek where it looks like she's battled a trash panda. Her rose stained lips are turned up in a pensive smile that reflects inward as she climbs the last boulder to reach my yard.

That boulder that may as well have a *keep out* sign attached to it for its aggressive profile.

At least she's wearing sturdy boots as she traverses the thin trail that leads toward my cabin after she climbs as though that's her only destination with a few days to go until Christmas. But it's the quick glance as she checks over her shoulder like she expects there to be traffic on this deserted road of mine and the haunted look in her pretty, sky blue eyes when she turns back my way that grips me at stomach level and refuses to let go.

Christ. What sort of bait is she that she's out here alone and fucking miles from anywhere?

Answer: the sort that I want to take hold of and find out what the hell she's doing here and why she's on my land.

Which means it's time to show my hand.

Lowering my rifle a fraction, I step away from the hide I've been resting behind and let her see me. She freezes, widening those pretty eyes framed with thick lashes. Her hands splay at her sides. Breaths come short before they stall altogether. I can almost taste her panic, relish the way she wants to bolt, because I'll chase her down and we both know it.

She won't make it as far as the Red Cedar that's just beyond my place before I take her to the ground beneath me and start my interrogation. The thought of finding out what those curves feel like first hand against my skin is enough to send blood roaring south a second time.

"Here, kitty, kitty," I murmur, just to antagonize the shit out of her as I lower my rifle a little more.

Enough to give myself freedom to chase her when she runs.

Enough to let her think she has a chance if she does.

Her feet angle towards my cabin like she thinks she might beat me there and lock me out. It's cute, the tiniest signs of hope she displays.

"You live here?" she calls, her voice loud enough to bounce off the granite rocks around me.

Defiant and sassy as all hell.

I love her attitude. This is going to be fun.

"This is private property." I suppose I'm supposed to put on a show of humanity or some other bullshit around what's probably a local girl or some tourist out to climb the mountains.

In winter. With snow coming on that's been holding off for a week or more this season already.

Christ. She must have a death wish.

Where the hell is her pack?

"People don't usually come out here."

There's a reason I'm out this far on my own, honey. A man like me isn't fit for human consumption.

Especially not for a woman like you.

She might have figured that out on her own by now. Not that it seems to deter her.

"People might not, but I do. I'm looking for someone."

I quirk an eyebrow. "Not anyone else is out here to be found."

"Who says I'm looking for anyone else?" The sassy tone is back in her voice.

That sass calls to me like honey.

I'm so fucked just looking at her that it takes a

moment too long for her words to register. "Why are you out here?" My rifle rises. I relax my grip with effort.

That rifle has been an extension of my arm for decades. It kept me safe in deserts that contain sand that's a different color to this country. Shit, I can still taste that pink dust on the back of my tongue on nights when it's snowing outside and too damn damp for grit to be fucking anywhere. But it's damn well there anyway.

That rifle stayed with me all the way home. I nursed it on my lap right next to the box that held my best friend. The only time I put it down was to kneel before his mother and beg her forgiveness.

Then I brought my ass up north and walked away from the rest of the world.

I've been here ever since, and that rifle has saved my life countless times. Kept me fed, too. Now, that same rifle feels heavy in my grip. For the first time, I wonder if I've been holding on to it too tightly.

"Who are you looking for, honey?" I ask softly.

Too softly.

Her chin rises.

She's all sass and filthy from her walk up my mountain. Dirty in all the right sort of ways. When she pops a hip with the sort of smile that promises sin, my blood runs hot despite my inner reflections.

The effects this woman has on me, when I don't even know her name, is insanity itself.

"You're Gabriel Decker, right?" She watches me carefully.

I nod slowly. She knows my name. That's... something new. A game changer for sure. I keep my grip on my rifle all the same.

"That's right." *Just because you know who I am doesn't stop me from wanting to play, honey.*

"Good." Her feet plant firmly in the hard packed dirt before me. "Because I'm sick of walking. I need your help."

I huff a laugh under my breath. Who in the hell has this woman been talking to in Hope Peak that gave her the impression that I'm one of the good guys? Because I'm sure as hell not one. She can keep thinking that if she likes. It'll mean a cute surprise for both of us.

Merry fucking Christmas to me.

READ **MOUNTAIN MAN'S LOVE AT FROST SIGHT.**

ABOUT THE AUTHOR

USA Today Bestselling author Sofia Aves writes fast-paced police romances, sizzling military units, steamy cowboys with a Montana backdrop and the occasional cheeky god. Sofia writes kidlit for charity and has over one hundred and fifty publications across five not-so-super-secret pen names. As acquisitions editor for Evernight and Evernight Teen publishing she loves discovering new talent in romance and YA spaces, and is a mum of three crazies in a returned veteran household. Sofia has two overly large fur babies who think they're teacup puppies, a duck who prefers to eat from a dog bowl and two axolotls named after a dragon and a firebird.

Sofia lives near Brisbane, Australia, where she has her own alpaca park, Lorendel.

www.sofiaaves.com

Sign up to <u>Sofia's newsletter</u> and get a free Blue Blooded Brothers book.

Haven't read the Z Boy's prequel? Get it for free here:
A TABLE FOR TEN
Follow Sofia on
BookBub
Twitter
Instagram

READ SOFIA'S SERIES

Link

Blue Blooded Brothers

Collision

Politics & Paperwork

Blindsided

Sentinel

Mugshots & Candy Canes

Impact

Reckoning

Red Hart Ranch

Snow on the Range

Siren on the Range

Sundown on the Range

Spirit on the Range

Ash on the Range

Mistletoe on the Range

Forgotten Mountain Man

Forsaken Mountain Man

Texan Devils

Ranger's Wish

Ranger Bedevilled

Ranger's Passion

Ranger's Fury

Ranger's Wrath

Ranger's Storm

Snapdragons & Seductions

Summer with a Ranger

Merry with a Ranger

Beach Duty Collection

Playing to Win

Off Boarding

Vicious Slash

Zero Pointer

Off Stage Fling

Rippton Allstars

Crushing It

Glacial Force

Rippton Creatives

Study Games

Make Me, Break Me

Twisted Obsession

Spring Break with a Mafia Prince

A Royally Fake French Menage

Angel Shot

Jericho Chimeras

Puck Me Always

<u>Puck My Prey</u>

Puck My Heart

Puck me Sideways

Ridin' Horns

Kickin' Up Dust (coming 2026)

Saddling Up With My Bodyguard

Mountain Man's Love at Frost Sight

Z Boys

King

Joker

Hearts

Ace

Mayhem & Mistletoe

Ruski

Fast Track to Love

Speed Trap

Klauss Brothers

Zander

Keegan

Gallo Empire *with Jade Marshall*

Splintered Vows

Fractured Vows

Fierce Vows

Savage Covenant

Rom Coms

She's A Hot Christmas Mess

Boats, Moats and Root Beer Floats

Writing Romantasy as

SOFIA SHELLEY

Dead Poets Sorority

Writing Reverse Harem Dark Romance as

DOVE PRIEST

Recurve Ridge

Kidlit writing as

JO SEYSENER

The OCD Elf

The OCD Elf's Great Reindeer Calamity

Greg and the Egg

writing YA as

JOSS PHOENIX

Alchem Academy

HIDE FROM US

Writing spicy paranormal romance as
RAVEN HUSH
Club Fray
Darkest Desires
Purge
Kidnapped By Claws
Ruin
Shadow Lords
Sinner's End
Heaven's Gate (2026)
Monster Brides
Phoenix's Eternal Flame
Kraken's Vow
Krampus' Christmas Bride
Silent Sentinels Duet
Reflections of Silence
Echoes in the Void
Monsters In New York
Feral Moon Rising
Dark Water Refuge